CW00455831

Return to Linstowel

Return to Linstowel

SUSAN SALLIS

ROBERT HALE · LONDON

ISBN 0 7090 6156 0

Robert Hale Limited
Clerkenwell House
Clerkenwell Green
London EC1R 0HT

2 4 6 8 10 9 7 5 3 1

Printed in Great Britain by
St Edmundsbury Press Limited, Bury St Edmunds, Suffolk.
Bound by WBC Book Manufacturers Limited, Bridgend.

ONE

ABBIE had been coldly nervous all the way down on the train. Memories of her holiday visit to Linstowel two years ago had been brutally squashed by this superficial fear and she had walked down the long combe to the village without once thinking of Mark or Christopher or her younger self, so happy—almost smugly happy— in the security of her little family.

Now, suddenly, in the neat school house, with the present teacher's slippers just visible beside the brass coal hod, her nerves disappeared. She was still cold in spite of the June sunshine which made the old-fashioned mahogany furniture shine darkly, but it was the cold of complete detachment now. She could almost split herself into two people, one of whom could stand aside and watch the other one sitting there with the two younger applicants for the job, chatting artificially about the difficulties of running a one-teacher school in these days of free activity and integrated time-tables. It was ten years since she had taught and things had changed. Some of the phrases the others used meant nothing to her. There she sat, her pale, flyaway hair confined under an unaccustomed hat, her dark blue linen suit and gloves immediately marking her as old-fashioned compared with the casual dresses and carefully groomed bare heads of the younger teachers.

She knew which one she would have chosen to teach Christopher. The one with the dark blue laughing eyes and the low, humorous voice. She was barely out of college and still full of enthusiasm and new ideas. A far better guide and companion for a lively eight-year-old boy than a woman well into her thirties, doubtless with out-of-date ideas on education and with personal reasons for wanting this lonely job that had nothing much to do with the good of any future pupils.

Her detachment was so complete that she could no longer really remember just why she had applied for the position of head teacher at Linstowel Primary in the first place. It seemed now to have been a thoughtless, even a selfish move to have made. Was it because she had spent a holiday here two years ago and had been happy? She should had learned by now that you could never turn the clock back and that to revisit old haunts did nothing but inflict pain. So why? Of course, there had been the fact that she and Mark and Chris had helped a small family who were then in the same boat as she was now. But what exactly did that imply? Surely she didn't expect them to pay her back in kind— even if they still lived here?

She discovered she had tied her gloves into a reef knot. The young teacher with the blue eyes grinned at her.

"Nervous?" she said.

Abbie smiled back. "Not any more. As a matter of fact I've started to wonder why on earth I'm here."

6

The door opened and from the tiny study which was today's interview room, the Reverend Odgers, Chairman of the School Managers, emerged looking like a benevolent crow.

"Miss Barker?"

The other girl, dark-haired and vivacious, stood up.

"We are taking you in alphabetical order, ladies. That means Mrs Eliot will be next, and you, Miss Purbright"—he gave the blue-eyed girl a special smile—"will be last."

Behind him the study was cram-full with people. Miss Barker squeezed past the portly stomach and took the vacant Windsor chair by the window, and the door closed gently upon her.

"He's sweet," Miss Purbright said, looking fondly at the door. "I went to his service at Castle Combe last Sunday and introduced myself in the porch afterwards, and he invited me to the vicarage to have coffee and meet his wife."

Abbie was amazed. "Is that allowed? I mean—"

"It does seem a bit underhand, I agree. But you see, they don't know any of us personally—only what we've told them in those application form things. So it helps them if they've met us socially. Jobs down here are very difficult to get."

"Yes, I know. I'm surprised though that you and Miss Barker would consider burying yourself in such a tiny place. It will be terribly dull all through the winter, surely?"

"Well . . . it's only thirty miles from Casterbridge of

7

course. That's my home." Abbie thought thirty miles
sounded a long way on a dark winter's night after a
full day at school. "My boy friend's got a Mercedes,"
Miss Purbright added, looking down her long nyloned
legs to one pointed toe. Abbie wondered whether after
all she would have opted for Miss Purbright to teach
Christopher.

And suddenly, as so often happened, her breath
caught in her throat. A teacher for Christopher . . . if
only. . . .

They sat silently. From outside the sound of children
bursting into the playground came to their ears. Abbie
smiled reminiscently, somehow restored by the cheerful
babble. There would be milk for the little ones and a
quick coffee for the teacher by an open doorway, and a
succession of confidences and complaints. "Look at this
empty snail-shell, miss. Where has the snail gone?" . . .
"That big boy came and spoiled our game, miss . . ."
The sun was hot and some of the less hardy ones would
want to sit in the shade of the big elm, and perhaps the
little girls would play house there . . . children didn't
change. Abbie felt her smile deepen. Was this her reason
for coming back? The unchangingness of children? But
then, why here, so far away in tiny Linstowel?

Miss Purbright cleared her throat. "I just thought. I
suppose she—" An elegant finger stabbed in the direction
of the school ."I suppose there's no playtimes for her? I
mean, she must have to do continuous playground duty?"

"Yes. And dinner duty. We won't have much chance
to talk to her."

"Quite." Miss Purbright made a face, obviously thinking of other things besides an informative chat with the present teacher.

The study door opened again and Miss Barker came back into the sitting-room, smiling thanks over her shoulder. Abbie began to gather up her handbag, but the door closed again.

"They want a few moments to chat me over," the dark girl explained, flopping exhausted into a chair. "What a grilling! Actually I'm not too sure I want their blessed job now. They're terribly formal in their educational ideas and there's something fishy about it all."

"Fishy?" Miss Purbright pounced.

"I don't know—I could be absolutely wrong. I got the feeling they expected me to run the school as if it were a beleaguered fort."

"No outings or trips, do you mean?" prompted Miss Purbright. "Probably the few families down here are very hard up and can't manage any extras."

"Well, I don't know. It's just a feeling. There's one man there, I think he's the important one. His name's Lampton. He keeps chipping in with completely irrelevant questions."

Abbie vaguely remembered the name. There was a big farm out on the cliff road, simply called the Lampton place.

"What sort of questions?" asked Miss Purbright curiously and not quite so avidly. Abbie sensed her cooling attitude.

"Well, he suddenly asked me if I could mend a fuse.

9

I was in the middle of explaining about the Initial Teaching Alphabet—"

"Do they use that reading method?" Abbie asked. She had never met I.T.A. either at college or at her teaching posts afterwards.

"No. And they don't like it either."

"Anyway, Mr Lampton's not the chairman," Miss Purbright said almost defiantly. "Surely Mr Odgers isn't so—factual?"

Before Miss Barker could reply the study door opened again and the kindly crow smiled at Abbie.

"You're next, Mrs Eliot. Would you like to come in?"

Abbie side-stepped past him and into the study, where Miss Liddell and her predecessors must have sat for many hours working out lesson plans and marking books. She felt a momentary sense of unreality again, this time as if the last ten years of her life had never happened and she was Miss Hart again on her first interview. She sat in the Windsor chair and looked around her. Mr Odgers still hovered solicitously—Miss Purbright was right in saying he was sweet because he offered her a cushion and asked whether the open window was too much for her.

"Such a beautiful day," she murmured, placing the small, wiry man as Mr Lampton and the upright woman as Lady Margaret from the Hall. There was another man, tall and thin.

"I was thinking of the noise from the playground," Mr Odgers insisted, still standing by the open sash.

She smiled up at him. "I should hardly be here if I

found children's voices unendurable," she said, wondering whether his thoughtfulness had a deeper motive.

He smiled back. "Quite. Now, Mrs Eliot, you will realise that in many ways this interview is unusual."

He waited and she felt constrained to make some reply. "I have never been interviewed without the head teacher being present."

"Quite," said Mr Odgers again. "Actually we have a retired head teacher in Mr Dawes—" He indicated the tall, thin man next to him. "But obviously Miss Liddell is not present. For one thing she cannot be spared from the children. For another, though we have every respect for her, she is leaving us, and her opinion is felt to be —er—somewhat—"

"Superfluous," snapped Mr Lampton, hitching himself impatiently in his chair. "Could we get on, Vicar? There's work waiting for me."

Lady Margaret and Mr Dawes permitted themselves small smiles at this brusqueness. The inference that Mr Odgers, who was the only one there besides Lampton young enough to be working, could be easily spared, was not quite obvious enough to be rude, but the vicar shot the small, wiry man rather an unchristian glance as he carried on.

"We see from your form that you are a widow, Mrs Eliot." Abbie almost held her breath in case he offered unctuous condolences, but he carried on levelly, "Have you taken any other position since you lost your husband?"

"No."

11

"Have you done no work outside your home since you left teaching ten years ago?"

"No."

Lampton leaned forward suddenly. His skin was red and shiny from the sun and his nose hooked like Punch's.

"You've coped alone the last year, Mrs Eliot?"

"Of course."

"What I meant was—you haven't lived with a relative —your mother perhaps?"

"My parents are dead. I've lived alone."

"It took you a long time to decide to return to teaching," commented Lady Margaret almost to herself.

"No. I made up my mind almost immediately to teach again. But it took me a long time to put my house in order and sell it."

Before Abbie could dwell on those long lonely months, Lampton pounced again. "What do you mean—put your house in order?"

"Surely that's rather a personal question," protested Mr Odgers.

Abbie smiled at him. "Not really. It was a literal reply. I painted and papered and did minor repairs. Then in the spring I discovered the garden had gone to ruin."

Lampton looked quickly around at the others and then sat back.

"Good," he said gruffly.

Mr Odgers smiled again. "Mr Lampton is reminding us that if you take this post you will be on your own for long periods of time and any—er—knack—you might have acquired in house maintenance will come in very useful."

Abbie said, "I believe County Hall are very considerate with these one-teacher schools and send someone out immediately they get a call."

"Ah. Yes. We try to be self-supporting. As far as we can, of course."

Mr Odgers placed the tips of his fingers together and sat back. Mr Dawes leaned over him and picked up Abbie's application form from the table.

"You are perhaps a little out of touch with modern teaching methods, Mrs Eliot," he stated dryly and as a fact. "What do you know about the Initial Teaching Alphabet?"

"Nothing," said Abbie without apology.

"Have you an opinion you would like to offer?"

She thought about it. "That is difficult as I am ignorant of the method. I use formal phonetics myself, but together with flash cards and appropriate books. That way there is no unlearning to be done later on."

"Let us assume next term you have three new arrivals —five-year-olds—without any reading or number knowledge at all, and you have no materials ready to hand. How would you begin with them?"

Abbie began hesitantly. "We would talk. Find their interests. Probably their parents, homes, pets. We would draw these, count them, make up books which would have words and numbers around the same theme. I would make flash cards from their own drawings . . ." She went on to describe a scheme which would probably last half a term. Her confidence grew with her enthusiasm and she leaned forward as she described a child-made model of the village from matchboxes and pipe-cleaners. "Imagine the sorting and counting in such a model. We could take our work outside and count houses on our nature walks. . . ."

Mr Dawes' voice was drier still. "You must remember, Mrs Eliot, that you would also have four or five children between six and seven, half a dozen eight- and nine-year-olds, besides your top group."

"Yes," she said, deflated. "This is the part that I find worrying. I have worked with family groups before, but not such a wide age range."

"You could of course develop your infant scheme as an environmental study for the older children," Mr Dawes said unexpectedly. "In fact I would imagine it better from your point of view as well as the children's if you used the same theme throughout the school. At different levels naturally."

"Yes," said Abbie breathlessly. Was it possible she was being considered?

Lady Margaret said in her beautifully deep voice, "How do you feel about sewing, Mrs Eliot?"

Abbie nodded. "It is good for the tinies to learn such manipulative skills. And, of course, the older ones find great fulfilment from something so permanently accomplished."

"Would you object to me coming to school to take a class of embroidery?"

"Obviously I should be delighted with any help,"

14

Abbie said cautiously. Unqualified help was often a mixed blessing, but Lady Margaret had a certain no-nonsense air about her that Abbie approved.

"We like our boys to do gardening," put in Lampton pugnaciously.

Abbie looked at him calmly. "I approve of as wide a curriculum as possible. But for all the children. I would like girls *and* boys to try embroidery as well as gardening. I would also like all the children, even the little ones, to have an opportunity of cooking and playing a musical instrument."

She felt as if she had shown all her cards. Nobody said anything for a moment, then Mr Odgers cleared his throat and murmured, "Highly commendable."

Lampton said angrily, "We've got no money for cooking or buying instruments, Mrs Eliot. This is an old-fashioned—"

"County Hall can usually be persuaded to stretch the grant if it's for something worthwhile," Abbie put in.

"Leave County Hall where they are!" snapped Lampton.

"Also parents are very good about supplying ingredients, and I suppose there is a cooker in the school house? A group of children could use that while Lady Margaret is taking others for embroidery."

The upright figure snapped further to attention at the familiar use of her name. Only Mr Dawes had been introduced.

Abbie went on gently, "The three R's cannot stand alone, Mr Lampton. Everything we do involves counting and reading and making judgements. Therefore, the more we do, the more we exercise our three R's." She stared into the pale blue eyes, recognising her real opponent. "You will find if two parents send along money for recorders, others will follow suit very quickly. By Christmas most of them will play two or three carols and there is a school orchestra. It is money well spent."

Mr Dawes was smiling quietly. Abbie knew she had won him over.

Lady Margaret said, "You seem to know us all by name, Mrs Eliot. Perhaps Miss Barker mentioned— though I do not believe we were introduced."

Abbie said frankly, "I have been to Linstowel before, Lady Margaret. Two years ago. The weather was like this. You opened the Midsummer Fete at the Lampton Place."

"I see." The far-seeing grey eyes looked piercingly at Abbie. "A sentimental return. To happier times."

Lampton made a noise of disgust in his throat.

"I don't know," Abbie answered truthfully. "At the time—it simply seemed the right thing to do."

Lady Margaret looked hard at Lampton and he said nothing.

"Very well then." Mr Odgers stood up. The interview was over. "We will let you know after lunch, Mrs Eliot. We are having a school lunch, of course, and hope you will join us."

Abbie murmured acquiescence and was back in the sitting-room, exhausted. The other two looked at her expectantly, waiting to hear her impressions, but she felt unable to sort them out for herself, let alone these girls. She felt herself swinging crazily between wanting to run away, back to her hotel at Casterbridge and then to the cramped flat, and wishing she could stay here in this small, friendly sitting-room and make another home. Different from the one she had had, blessedly different, but a home.

Miss Barker was saying, "I don't think I can bear a school lunch, do you? I noticed a gorgeous little inn down by the harbour—the Lobster Pot or something. Shall we explore?"

Abbie shook her head quickly. It would be the most natural thing in the world to go in there for one of their ploughman's lunches and say, "You don't remember me? I was here with my husband and son two years ago. . . ."

She said aloud, almost tersely, "I think we're expected to stay and eat with the children. They will want to see how we get on with them."

Miss Purbright nodded. "We'll have to stay. We can have a walk round after. My boy friend is coming for me later and he'll give you both a lift back to Casterbridge if you like."

Miss Barker accepted gladly, but Abbie smiled and reserved her answer. She knew that once the managers announced their decision she would have to escape quickly whatever it was. She dared not have any idle hours in Linstowel.

Playtime was long over, but a few voices could be

heard talking outside the sitting-room window. Miss Purbright was called in for her interview and Abbie stood up.

"I think I'll go and talk to those children outside," she said. "Coming?"

The dark girl shook her head. "No, thanks. I shall be facing my class again tomorrow. And next term, too, if I don't get this job."

Abbie smiled sympathetically and went into the tiny neat kitchen and through the open back door which led straight on to the playground. Two boys and two girls were giant-striding across the asphalt; another boy played with a trundle wheel. He straightened up when he saw her and called out, "How y'doing, Stan?"

One of the boys, an eight-year-old with a shock of red hair, stopped in mid-stride and looked confused.

"You great fool! You've made me forget where I got to—"

They all noticed Abbie at the same time.

She said, "Good morning children. You're measuring the playground?"

There was a ragged "Good morning, miss," then the red-headed Stan said more informally, "We *were* until Mister Paul Enys interrupted." Abbie recognised the boy with the trundle wheel and felt a shock of surprise. Of course, she had never seen him without his twin, but would that account for the change in him? The dark eyes were unaltered, but there was an anger emanating from his small person.

"Are you our new teacher, miss?" breathed one of the

girls. "I'm Rita Lampton, and I'm in the top reading group."

"My name's Letty Moran—"

"I'm Stan Burrows. This is Peter Edgehill—"

Paul Enys kicked the trundle wheel. "You'll never be able to tell me from my twin. We drive Miss Liddell round the bend—"

"Are you measuring with the trundle wheel?" Abbie said, ignoring the enquiries about her status and resisting the impulse to ask Paul whether he remembered her.

He gave her a sidelong look, suddenly vacant. "I dunno."

One of the girls giggled. The boys looked at Abbie and she realised they were waiting to see how she would cope with Paul's assumed idiocy.

She said briskly, "I expect these four are measuring in strides like the old Romans used to do. That will be about a yard. And you're going to get the exact measurement in yards with that wheel."

Letty giggled again and little Rita Lampton—surely not *that* Lampton's daughter—smiled congratulation.

"You're right, miss. Only every time we get halfway along"—she shot a dark look at Paul—"we get interrupted."

"I should get on with it now then," Abbie suggested, and was glad when the four striders immediately went into action without any further discussion. She hadn't lost her technique in that way. Paul Enys was another matter; it was easy to spot a trouble-maker in a class and she did not need Paul's defiant scuffling with the trundle

19

wheel to tell her where trouble lay in this school. Yet two years ago he had been such an amenable little boy. He and his twin, Peter, had played for hours with Chris and no quarrelling or unpleasantness at all. And they had only been six years old then. Her heart was squeezed with dreadful familiarity. Here was Paul Enys, now eight years old. An age Chris Eliot would never see.

She said gently, so that the others could not hear, "Actually I usually give this job to two people, Paul, so you must be a very sensible boy to cope with it alone."

Paul forgot to be stupid, flushed at the compliment and said quickly, "So you *are* the new teacher?"

"Perhaps. May I try the wheel? You'd better count up the yards though. I can't do both jobs." She put her back to the school wall and began trundling slowly. Paul looked completely blank. Either he didn't know how to use the trundle wheel or this was part of his anti-school campaign. Or anti-adult campaign. Either way it was anti-social and just did not belong to the Paul Enys she had known. She wondered why . . . and just how far it had gone. The wheel clicked loudly and she said, "You nearly missed that one, Paul . . . two . . . three . . . count them aloud please, otherwise we shall forget where we are."

He picked up the idea immediately and counted out the forty-five yards of the playground. The others were licking pencils and writing down their own results. She left them to compare notes, smiled briefly at Paul, and walked on round the playground, beneath the shady old elm, to the picket fence of the school-house garden.

Beneath some arthritic apple trees two older boys were doing a little desultory weeding. Abbie drew back against the wall of the house, not wishing to talk to any more of the children. She worked it out quickly; two of the top group here, four middle group doing practical maths in the playground, so probably Miss Liddell was telling a story or doing some reading work with the younger children. It would take a lot of organising, there would be a great deal of planning each evening, no time to think of anything else. . . .

Lady Margaret's distinctive voice came through the open window on her left. "I cannot imagine the young teachers welcoming me into the classroom . . . not of course that that has anything to do with my choice—"

"They're full of new ideas, however. Miss Purbright especially . . ." Mr Odgers' voice faded diffidently and then someone banged a fist on the table. Abbie could guess who it was.

Lampton's strong country voice said plainly, "Mrs Eliot has my vote. She's not going to fly off to get married or meet any young men. And she can cope with any little emergencies without getting on the phone to County Hall—"

"She won't be easily recruited to our partisan ideas," Mr Dawes said judiciously.

"I thought you were for her?" Lampton accused.

"Her teaching methods are mine. I think she will be completely conscientious. But if she believes our course is wrong, then she is capable of acting on her own initiative. That is all I am saying."

21

Abbie moved away quickly. Lampton and Lady Margaret for her and apparently the vicar and head master against. She hadn't imagined it would be like that. And Miss Barker was right. There was something odd about this appointment. Even, to use Miss Barker's word, fishy.

She walked slowly back to the kitchen door and the tiny twinkling sitting-room. For the hundredth time she wondered whether she was doing the right thing. Selling up her home had seemed inevitable. She could no longer have lived there alone. Taking up teaching again had been the obvious thing to do; she had to work at something and teaching was all-absorbing. But her determination to begin afresh, had that been sensible? And in fact in applying for Linstowel, was she really beginning afresh or was she trying to go back to the past? Or was she even drawn by the memory of a person more unhappy than herself?

She re-entered the sitting-room just as the school managers came smiling out of the study. The room was very crowded. Mr Dawes immediately sat on a stool by Miss Barker and asked her whether she intended swimming later on this afternoon. Lady Margaret stood with her back to the empty fireplace in what Abbie imagined was a typical pose. Lampton walked to the window and looked down the garden path to the road running on down the combe and into the village. He kept his back studiously to the rest of the room. Mr Odgers, as chairman and host, suggested a glass of sherry before lunch.

"Miss Liddell cannot be here to look after us, of

course, but she extends her welcome to you all and I am in *loco parentis* as it were." He chuckled fruitily and went to the mahogany sideboard to dispense drinks. Lampton shook his head and Lady Margaret accepted a small glass with intense suspicion. Everyone else relaxed slightly and talked about the weather. Abbie wondered whether these people would soon become welcome familiars, or whether they were all just ships passing her by as everyone had been since the crushing blow last year. She thought of the children she had just met in the playground. She could become fond of them. It might be that Paul Enys needed help and that she could supply it. If she didn't get the job, was she going to call into the Lobster Pot?

"Will you go swimming before you return home, Mrs Eliot?"

The talk about swimming had become general and Lady Margaret was trying to draw her into it.

She shook her head, smiling. "I have to be either very relaxed or very spartan to go swimming," she said. "And I am neither today."

Lady Margaret actually smiled and looked more like a horse than ever. "Not too tense I hope, my dear, we really are such ordinary people."

Abbie considered. "I am no more tense than usual, Lady Margaret. And I don't think any of you are . . . ordinary."

The aristocratic eyebrows shot up. The sherry glass was replaced on the sideboard half full. Then the level grey eyes met Abbie's and Lady Margaret said, "I should like to think we were jumping the same fence together, Mrs Eliot."

Abbie smiled her appreciation. She suddenly found herself hoping that Lady Margaret was not a ship that would pass in the night.

School lunch was the usual rather slapdash affair on a smaller scale than most schools. Abbie counted seventeen children and guessed that perhaps two or even three went home to lunch. Only one dinner lady was assigned to such a small school and the meals arrived in a van from kitchens in Casterbridge. The children sat around the infants' tables; varnished wood, Abbie noticed, instead of the usual rigid plastic surfaces found in most present-day classrooms. She made up her mind that if she got this job, her first sewing class would make gay gingham table-cloths for lunch-times and perhaps even the infants' milk. And it would take no time to have a jar of flowers on each table . . . she stopped herself quickly. She had no idea of the bulk of work Miss Liddell had to get through and her mental improvements implied a criticism she had no right to make. She kept her eyes studiously away from the bare window ledges and bitty walls. After all, Miss Liddell was leaving to get married and the end of term was only a few weeks away; why should she make more work for herself by mounting displays of the children's work?

After lunch, the dinner lady sat under the elm tree and the children played around her while Miss Liddell took them all back to the house for coffee. She was a tall, rather elegant girl of about twenty-six, delighted to be able to talk shop. Abbie realised for the first time how frustrating it must be to miss out on the co-operative discussions of a normal staff room. A large part of making a classroom look well and work well was the competitive spirit among keen staff. Miss Liddell had only been at Linstowel for a year and was obviously glad to be leaving it. Miss Barker and Miss Purbright began to look depressed.

At one-fifteen she left them alone again while she tidied up for her afternoon session. As the kitchen door closed behind her, an uneasy silence fell in the sunny room. Mr Dawes moved away from Miss Barker and ranged himself alongside Mr Lampton, and Mr Odgers cleared his throat several times while he glanced at his fellow managers.

"We have almost reached a decision on our side, ladies," he began, obviously receiving some invisible signal from the others. "But before we have any further interviews, we would like to put all of you into the picture. It may well affect *your* decisions, in which case our job could be simplified." Lampton fidgeted and Mr Odgers said hastily, "Or, of course, complicated still further."

The two young teachers exchanged glances and Abbie wondered half in horror and half in amusement, whether the job would be hers by default.

"Linstowel is a dying village, I very much regret to say. But a village with a stoical character and a determination to stay alive as long as possible." Mr Odgers did not take this very seriously. He smiled and received

smiles from the two youngsters. The other managers
looked grim. "As Miss Purbright knows, my main parish
is at Castle Combe and I can only take Evensong at
Linstowel on alternate Sundays. My curate copes with
the rest and I have an excellent lay preacher in Mr
Dawes." He nodded at the retired head master. It was
obvious he had given up Linstowel as lost already. "Our
school is also running down. The fabric is in poor condition and the building is heated by an old-fashioned
stove in winter—by the way, Lampton, the blacksmith
will have to be called in about that." Mr Lampton made
a note in a much-thumbed book. "Many parents prefer
to send their children to Castle Combe or Casterbridge,"
Mr Odgers went on. "So that our numbers are low." He
looked at the worn carpet. "Also this school house is not
equipped as we should like. There is no refrigerator, nor
central heating—none of the mod. cons. most of us have
come to rely upon."

Mr Lampton said brusquely, "It's a home and independence. Something many people crave for these days."

"Quite, quite. I am putting the black side of the
picture. The fact is, ladies, we need a teacher of . . .
of . . . resourceful independence here, who will be happy
to put up with . . . perhaps . . . less than the best in
order to keep our school going. Our parents are co-
operative and we manage very well indeed on our tiny
grant—"

"We do our own repairs," Lampton snapped. "Plumb-
ing, the lot."

Mr Dawes said gently, "County Hall is looking for a

reason to close us down, ladies. We have to be very careful to keep our standards high and at the same time to ask for no assistance."

Lady Margaret said, "Miss Liddell would have liked an infant helper. Of course there is no question of that. I can come in twice a week myself and we have a very good cleaner."

The three teachers stared at the four managers. Positions had suddenly reversed and the applicants had the upper hand. Abbie felt sorry for them. They were fighting a losing battle.

"I take it the children have to go to Casterbridge or Castle Combe at the age of eleven anyway?" she reminded them.

"Quite. We're not exactly isolationist, Mrs Eliot. We would like to keep the character of the countryside."

Mr Dawes said, "A village school. It still has relevance to the community and the children, do you not agree, Mrs Eliot?"

Abbie thought of Paul Enys. If he was losing his way, then he stood more hope of finding it again here than at Castle Combe, fifteen miles away.

She nodded vigorously. "In any case, small children must feel secure in order to learn anything, and they stand a better chance of security in their own village."

"Quite, quite." Mr Odgers stood up briskly, as if a decision had been reached. "We will retire to the study again, ladies, and see you again in the same order as before. Please feel you can ask us—anything."

He ushered Miss Barker into the study and opened

the window a little more. The others crowded in after him and the door closed.

Miss Purbright said in a low, urgent voice : "I don't want it. I hadn't bargained on the loneliness, and now this . . . I don't think Jenny Barker will want it either. So it'll be up to you."

Sure enough, Miss Barker was only out of the sitting-room for a brief five minutes, just long enough to have made her excuses. Abbie sat in her empty chair with a feeling that her own freedom of decision had been taken away from her. Suddenly it was no longer a question of whether this move was a good one from her own angle; indeed it seemed as if it might be far from good; but those children out in the playground, these people in here, even this dear little house . . . maybe they needed her. Not as Mark and Chris had needed her, of course. That could never be again . . .

Strangely, it was Lampton who spoke first. His face, brick-red now from the heat in the close study, turned on her almost pleadingly, "Well, Mrs Eliot?"

"Come now, Lampton," protested Mr Odgers. "Mrs Eliot will have questions for us—"

"She knows her own mind," Lampton said.

Abbie smiled at the Punch-like face of the farmer. He had no polish and made no attempt to hide his impatience, but she would never forget he had voted for her from the outset.

"My application stands, Vicar," she said directly. "I understand your difficulties and I am afraid that in the end you will lose your school, especially if other parents decide to remove their children. But I would like to keep it going for as long as possible."

"That's that, then," said Lampton, and Lady Margaret murmured, "Bravo."

Mr Odgers glanced at them. "We still have to see Miss Purbright, of course. Perhaps you could wait, Mrs Eliot?"

Another five minutes trickled by. Miss Barker had already left, and Abbie walked around the sitting-room and tried to believe it might be hers.

Miss Purbright came out of the study and made a face at Abbie.

"Good luck," she whispered, and then aloud, "I'm going to join Jenny Barker on the beach until our lift arrives. Are you sure—?"

"Quite." Abbie smiled her thanks and farewell. Mr Odgers was at the front door, expressing regret and good wishes for her future. The others were talking urgently in the study. Lady Margaret was the first to come out and she immediately mounted guard over the fireplace. "Congratulations, Mrs Eliot. I hope you will be happy with us."

"It is definite then?"

"The other two have withdrawn their applications. But there is no question of re-advertising. We had already decided to offer you the position."

Abbie smiled. "It is generous of you to tell me so."

The others came and sat down comfortably in the sitting-room. There was a lot to discuss. A list of repairs to the school and school house. Coke to be ordered for the school stove, coal for the cottage. A possibility of having the kitchen and bathroom painted if Mrs Eliot would care to help with the cost? The boatyard had some planed wood which must be collected for the carpentry corner. Lady Margaret would bring embroidery silks and Mr Dawes had a waste-paper contact who could supply drawing and rough paper. . . .

"No money for materials either?" Abbie asked, daunted.

Mr Dawes smiled. "The more you can save the better, Mrs Eliot. The blacksmith will have to be paid for seeing to the stove, and the floor in the infants' corner is getting splintery and will need professional sanding."

"I have a perfectly good cord carpet we could use," Abbie suggested. Lampton smiled at her again.

The school bell rang to warn parents that their children would soon be arriving home. It was a signal for the managers to leave, too. Lady Margaret put on her mannish hat and Mr Odgers took her arm. Mr Dawes shook hands. "Telephone me when you're installed in the cottage, I'll be happy to help in any way I can."

She walked to the door with him and watched him climb the combe road to his retirement bungalow on the cliff. Children crowded the lane. How strange that so soon they would all be familiar to her.

Suddenly, amidst the sea of children, she saw a familiar figure, and her hand went up in greeting. It was Daniel Enys, landlord of the Lobster Pot, who had seemed to enjoy Mark's company so much during that wonderful holiday. He didn't see her, his eyes were searching the children.

"Dad!" It was Paul Enys, yelling stridently. "Dad! Can we have some sweets at Gran's? Dad—" Peter hung on to his brother's blazer as he fought a way through the crowd. Daniel stood still and silent, waiting for them. Nobody else spoke to him. In spite of the milling children and his own two sons reaching out to him, Abbie thought he looked unbearably lonely. She half lifted her hand again to wave.

"That's one member of our community—" Lampton was standing behind her, deliberately mimicking Mr Dawes' precise tones and words, "—who is a little less than co-operative."

"Oh?" Abbie dropped her hands and turned towards him. He was shorter than she was, bowed and jockey-like. She wondered if his physical appearance accounted for his aggressiveness.

"He owns the Lobster Pot. Could bring visitors into the place if he made it a little more attractive. But he's gone downhill over the last couple of years or so."

"I believe he lost his wife, Mr Lampton," Abbie said quietly.

Lampton's head jerked up. "Oh. So he's another one you know down here, is he? An acquaintance like Daniel Enys won't do you any good in Linstowel, Mrs Eliot. That man is trouble—"

"I simply knew him as the landlord of the inn. We stayed there for two very short weeks and my son played with his children. That's all." Abbie was already regretting the impulse that had made her spring to Daniel's defence.

"Yes. Well, be careful, that's all. Remember, you only got the job because no-one else wanted it." He almost pushed past her and stumped down the steps to the lane.

She stared after him in disbelief. Could anyone really be as unpleasant as Mr Lampton? Yet he was the one who had come fully out on her side at the interview. And unfortunately she had the feeling that he was the one who got things done at Linstowel school.

She looked back down the lane for a last glimpse of Daniel. But he had gone, hurrying his two little boys, where? To their grandmother's? Two years ago there had been no one and they had turned to the Eliots for companionship and comfort. Presumably Daniel had brought his mother down here to help him. And yet, according to Lampton, he was going downhill. Something was wrong; that was plain from Paul's behaviour.

Sighing, Abbie turned back into the cottage that would soon be her own. She must make some arrangements with Miss Liddell and catch the four-thirty back to her hotel at Casterbridge.

TWO

I⊤ wᴀs nearly three months later when Abbie arrived
in Linstowel to take up her appointment. It had been
raining and blowing for three days; a cold rain for
August; and already some of the trees were shedding
their leaves. The platform was deserted and for a second
time that summer she read the scarred notice that said
Linstowel had been an unstaffed halt since 8th September 1968 and passengers could purchase their tickets on
the train. Soon no trains would stop here and that would
be another stage in the death of the village.

She stood still while the train pulled away and the
last coach trundled under the rusty iron footbridge and
round the bend. Then she was alone with her case
beside her and the wind coming straight across the
Atlantic blowing leaves and rubbish around her sensible
brogues. She had a feeling, repeated over and over again
this last year, of burning her boats. Bit by bit, action by
action, she was making it impossible to return home to
the friends she and Mark had made.

She looked around. The shabby platform and derelict
waiting-room gave the Reverend Odgers' words a definite
meaning. Behind the derelict waiting-room a few palm
trees thrashed their leaves. Christopher had loved those.

33

He had called them desert-island trees and used their supple spears as swords. Beyond the trees was a fuschia hedge, thin and rusty as the footbridge, which followed the lane down the combe to the village and the sea. Nothing here to attract any but the most determined tourist; it was plain why Linstowel's children had to leave to find work.

Abbie pushed her heavy case into the waiting-room and patted her pocket to make sure the big old-fashioned front door key of the school house was there. Then she set off, avoiding the puddles with difficulty and bending her head against the wind.

There was just a week before the autumn term began; she had deliberately left her arrival as late as she dared so as to have no spare time on her hands. She had received an estimate for the painting in the school house and had agreed to it—it only amounted to part of the cost of the materials. Presumably the pugnacious Mr Lampton would have gone ahead with that, so that her precious bits and pieces from home, which would arrive early next week, could be moved in immediately. There would be plenty of settling in to be done besides getting ready for the new term. She wouldn't have a spare minute—with luck.

She was surprised to see the cottage windows still curtained—surely they had left with Miss Liddell—and a large pair of wellingtons standing in the front porch. Frowning slightly, she fitted the key into the door and pushed it open. The sitting-room was exactly as she remembered it, dull in the grey light of the rain-filled afternoon, but cosy with a small bowl electric fire standing in the grate drying a wet scarf which was draped over a tiny school chair. Abbie had an instant to take in the fact that the house was obviously occupied, when a voice sang out from the kitchen and Miss Liddell appeared in the doorway.

She looked completely confused at the sight of Abbie. "Mrs Eliot!" She whisked the headscarf and chair under the table. "I really am most awfully sorry. I wasn't expecting you until after the weekend."

Abbie was just as confused. "The weekend?" she repeated.

"Well . . . it's the Bank Holiday weekend—had you forgotten? And I came down for a break before the wedding. With my fiancé. I thought it might be him coming in. He's gone for a walk along the cliff." There was an awkward pause. Abbie was still holding the open front door and Miss Liddell did not ask her to come in. "Perhaps you would stay for tea?" she added belatedly.

Abbie was horrified. "I'd forgotten about the Bank Holiday," she confessed. "Actually I thought my tenancy had started at the end of last term. But I didn't come before because Mr Lampton was going to have some painting done."

Miss Liddell made a wry face. "He hasn't, I'm afraid. That's typical of him. He'll want to do everything in a rush the day before school starts. Or not at all. Actually my tenancy finishes on Saturday, but as there are no trains on a Sunday I didn't think you'd arrive till Monday. I've arranged to leave on Sunday afternoon."

She paused. "I'm terribly sorry no one told you . . . it's typical actually. You could stay here, but of course there's Harry . . ." She looked helplessly at Abbie.

"It's all right. Honestly. I'll find somewhere just for the three nights and move in here during Sunday afternoon." Miss Liddell still looked worried and it occurred to Abbie it could be for another reason. "Don't expect me at all, will you? I might have to go back to Casterbridge."

Miss Liddell only just hid her relief. Abbie began to back down the steps.

"Look, I really am sorry. We should have another talk really— I'll leave a note with any last-minute thoughts, shall I? I do feel awful—"

"What nonsense," said Abbie, nearly at the gate. "I should have telephoned and made certain . . . dreadful weather for the holiday weekend, isn't it?"

Somehow she was through the gate and hidden from the cottage by the fuschia hedge. She was appalled. It was nearly five o'clock and there were no trains back to Casterbridge after four-thirty. There might be buses to Castle Combe, but presumably no more hope of accommodation there than here.

For the first time in a year she had unplanned time on her hands. It was Thursday and she couldn't move in until Sunday. Three days of idleness and then there would not be enough time to do all she had to before school began. A pit of depression and uncertainty yawned before her and she dug her hands into the pockets of her raincoat and walked quickly on down the combe before it could swallow her.

One of the first shops in the little village street was the general store she and Chris and Mark had haunted two years before. She went inside. Paul and Peter Enys were busy choosing lollipops from the sweet counter. Quickly Abbie turned away and began to read a notice about a village social in the church hall on Saturday night. She had temporarily forgotten the problem of the Enys' and felt completely unable to face the two little boys at the moment. Behind her the children wrangled not quite amiably and a voice eventually told them to take their sweets into the back and sit and eat them until the rain gave over.

"Can I help you, madam? I'm sorry to keep you. The children have to take their time when they have only two and a half pence between them and starvation!"

Abbie didn't recognise the humorous face of the white-haired lady behind the counter. Which was strange because this was one of the shops they had haunted two years before.

"I wondered if you might know of a holiday flat or cottage vacant for the weekend." Abbie was suddenly conscious of not even having a handbag. She put up a hand and tucked a strand of wet hair under her headscarf.

The woman looked doubtful. "Most of them are let for the week, my dear. There's the Lobster Pot. There's plenty of room there."

At this time of the year when Daniel should be full? Abbie said diffidently, "I really wanted a place where I could please myself. With meals and so on."

The woman looked closely at her, then nodded. "Of course. I understand." It was almost as if she did. "My son might know of somewhere. I only came here last year. He runs the Lobster Pot—"

"Daniel Enys?" Abbie said, suddenly realising who this woman was.

"That's right. You know him? It amazes me the number of people that boy knows!" The woman gave another of her smiles. "He'll be calling in here any minute to check on me and the children—if you would like to sit down and wait."

But Abbie was already turning blindly to go, instinct taking over from good judgement. Her headscarf slipped back and her pale hair, damp and unmanageable, fell about her face. She felt completely dishevelled. "I really must try myself—perhaps later—"

But already Daniel Enys' burly frame was blocking the doorway and she realised that if she pushed past him she would be calling unwelcome attention to herself. What was the matter with her? Daniel was the obvious person to help her find accommodation—it was his business after all—and she had wanted to meet him again, hadn't she? She sank into the chair Mrs Eyns had indicated and tried to smooth her hair.

There was a little pause. Daniel Enys, bigger than she remembered in an oilskin over his old naval jersey, stayed where he was in the doorway staring at her. She wondered whether he didn't recognise her, or whether he himself did not wish to be recognised. She decided it best not to remind him of their acquaintance.

Mrs Enys frowned slightly, and then said in a deliberately ordinary voice, "Ah, Daniel, I was expecting you—" She paused again, obviously waiting for Abbie to introduce herself. Then she went on more formally, "I wondered if you might know of a flat for the weekend. We have an unexpected visitor to Linstowel—"

Daniel came on into the shop, apparently not recognising her. He lifted the counter-flap and joined his mother. Under the shop lights Abbie could see he had grown a beard. It made him look much older.

He said without much interest, "There's a couple of rooms at the inn—how many of you, Mrs—?"

"Eliot," said Abbie. "And I rather hoped—"

"Mrs Eliot needs to be by herself for a bit," Mrs Enys explained in a matter-of-fact voice that took embarrassment away.

Daniel drummed considering fingers on the counter. "It isn't often we're full down here, Mrs Eliot. But August Bank Holiday . . . there's Margo's cottage, of course."

"Would she mind?" Mrs Enys said doubtfully. "She's never let it before, has she?"

"No. But I've used it as an overflow from the hotel before now." He turned directly to Abbie, apparently making up his mind. "Miss Ritchie is a family friend. She has a cottage on the cliffs."

It was a statement, but Abbie shook her head quickly. "Really I couldn't dream—I'll find bed and breakfast just for tonight—"

"Everywhere will be full—" Abbie wondered why on

39

earth he had spare rooms at the Lobster Pot. "I have the key of the cottage because I'm decorating the spare bedroom. You'll be all right at Margo's. She's an artist and the place is cluttered with canvases but that won't worry you." Again he was telling, not asking her. "It's right up on the cliff by itself—very quiet. Where's your luggage?"

"I left it at the station."

"We'll fetch it and go straight to the cottage." Ignoring her protests, he turned to his mother. "The twins watching television?"

"I hope so. I sent them into the parlour with their sweets. We really must talk some time, Daniel—"

"Of course," Daniel grinned. He was busy helping himself to tobacco—so he was still a pipe-smoker—and paying money into the till. "They'll grow up soon, Mother. Don't worry." He lifted the flap again. "My car's outside, Mrs Eliot—" He preceded her through the door, leaving no chance for argument, and walked around to the passenger side of the car.

Abbie actually recognised it. For the first time since her arrival she smiled at its comfortable familiarity. He noticed the smile.

"Yes. It's still the old Morris. It rarely goes wrong and there seems no point in changing it."

She sat rigidly while he came round the car and took his place behind the wheel. Then she said shakily, "You recognise me? Why didn't you say something straight away? I thought you'd forgotten—"

"Of course I knew you immediately, just as you knew

me. But if you wanted to be incognito . . . you don't
have to say a word, Abbie. Just sit and look out of the
window and stay in Margo Ritchie's cottage for a few
days. It doesn't matter that I know you and you know
me."

"But you must have thought it so odd—"

"What does it matter what I think—?"

"But I feel I should explain."

"No!" He shook his head abruptly. "Don't explain
anything. You never asked me for explanations, Abbie.
I appreciated that. Anyway, you wouldn't feel obliged
to explain if I were a stranger. Just because we knew
each other briefly two years ago doesn't mean you owe
me anything."

She was silent, grateful yet strangely rebuffed. What
was there to say if she didn't refer to the past or tell him
about Mark and Chris or the job at the school?

She said at last, "How are the boys?"

"Tearaways. You must have seen them in the shop.
They've run wild. My mother bought the business so
that she could be near them and lend a civilising influence, but she gets little time through the summer. I'll
probably send them to boarding school next year."

"No—" She spoke unguardedly. "Don't do that—"
She caught his sidelong glance and added lamely, "They
need you."

He gave a short laugh, unamused. "Like a sore head.
They need what is known as a steady environment."

She was silent, not wanting to appear curious after
his warning against explanations. He did not ask about

Mark or Christopher. He seemed to accept her solitary presence here as the most natural thing in the world.

He changed into low gear to begin the long climb up the combe. They passed the school and school house and Abbie spotted a tall young man shaking a macintosh in the front porch. She sighed.

"Are you certain it will be all right with the owner if I use her cottage? I don't want to do anything underhand." She had planned everything so carefully and was suddenly caught up in doubts at allowing herself to be taken off like this.

"I've known Margo for years. She was a friend of my wife's. She won't mind, believe me." He turned and flashed her a smile. "You won't see me working in the spare room. You won't hear me either, unless I drop a hammer on my toe."

She had to laugh, but it was a shock to realise he intended going on with his work while she was there.

They collected the case and drove back, then took a lane along the cliffs. The cottage stood alone in a field; not picturesque or beautiful itself, but commanding superb views from the front windows. Inside, the rooms were all whitewashed and almost frugally bare; there were no curtains or ornaments, just one good picture on the fireplace wall and stacks of canvases on the floor.

Daniel grinned. "What did I tell you. She's a Spartan. Her friends refuse to visit her in these surroundings so she wrote and asked me to pretty up the spare bedroom. You might be able to help actually. If you were interested."

It was as if he knew she had dreaded spare time to use up; the thought of prettying-up a room would have been ludicrous a couple of hours ago. Now, she nodded. "Perhaps I could."

He fetched logs to light a fire against the grey evening while she made tea in the tiny lean-to kitchen. There were just two of everything—mugs, spoons, plates. She had to wash a mug because he had made himself coffee that morning. She suddenly realised she had no perishable food. But there were plenty of stores; tea, coffee, sugar, dried milk, biscuits. She would manage till morning and walk down to Mrs Enys' shop.

"Come and look," Daniel said quietly behind her.

She followed him back into the living-room. The flames transformed the room into patterns of leaping light and shade and he had pulled the one armchair close to the grate. But it was to the window that he led her. Below them, the grey cloud was pierced by a single ray of the sun as it dropped towards the Atlantic. The sea was topped with white horses and pounded at the cliffs rhythmically. Abbie had forgotten the magnificence of the coast; in such a maelstrom of nature surely she could forget her puny self for a while?

She found she was gripping the window ledge fiercely. This was, after all, what she had come for. When she had seen the advertisement in the teaching magazine, Linstowel had meant Daniel Enys, and Daniel Enys had perhaps meant the only person on this earth who could fully understand. She hadn't talked—not really talked— to anyone since that dreadful night last year when the

43

police had brought her the news. There had been no one who could understand. So she had kept busy. Day after day . . . doing enough things to make her tired by midnight. And now, as if by a miracle, she had time to spare and she was with someone who had known her husband and son . . . and someone for whom the destitution of loss still meant something.

She said in a strangled whisper, "Daniel. I must tell you—"

His hand was almost brutal on her arm. "Be quiet, Abbie. I don't want to know. Just look at it. Don't let it stimulate any confidences you might regret tomorrow." He kept hold of her arm for a full minute, then he released her and said, "Good night. You'd better bring the sheets in and air them by the fire. No one's slept in the bed for a couple of months at least." He crossed to the back door and looked at the two steaming mugs of tea on the kitchen table. Then he shrugged. "Sleep well, Abbie."

She watched the old Morris negotiate the field track to the cliff lane. Then he was gone. He hadn't even stopped to drink his tea with her. She gradually relaxed her hold on the window ledge. After all, she was a stranger and Daniel probably dreaded an emotional scene. He had hidden his own grief well two years ago; perhaps he was right . . . whenever she had to put into words the fact of Mark and Christopher's death she invariably broke down. . . .

The next morning she awoke with a curious sensation of something waiting to be done. The wind had dropped and a light rain was falling, turning the sea to pewter grey and making the frothing waves look sullen. She cleared up the grate and re-lit the fire, drank more tea and ate some water biscuits. And still the feeling was mysteriously with her. There was the shopping to fetch from Linstowel and she wanted to walk down to the sea and feel its iron cold on her bare feet, and maybe work up an appetite with a really long walk along the cliffs to the next combe, but none of those things answered her special feeling.

Then she remembered, and with a small smile of anticipation she went along the hall to the second bedroom.

Naturally Daniel had chosen a flowery paper, mercifully a small pattern rather like an old-fashioned cotton print, and the paintwork was a deep apricot. The tin sat on a newspaper on the floor. "Gold Sunset" it was called, which was rather thoughtful as this room looked away from the setting sun and over the heather-clad hills.

She considered painting the single wooden chair and tea chest with it, then thought too much Gold Sunset might be—too much—so she decided on white. Probably she could get some white nylon from the village and make a skirt for the tea chest; maybe some rigid plastic for a top, and then if there was a mirror somewhere, the tea chest would become a passable dressing-table with heaps of storage space inside . . . she was almost enjoying herself.

Daniel passed her in the ancient Morris halfway along the cliff lane, but he just waved and carried on. She went on down the side of the combe, slipping a little in the muddy rain, enjoying the smell of the gorse and sea-pinks; conscious that the summer was ending. The small harbour was deserted and Daniel's inn crouched to one side of the slipway like a sleeping animal, though a thin curl of smoke from one chimney told of local life within its old oak and brass tap-room. How Chris had loved Daniel's tales of the smugglers who had really used the Lobster Pot in years gone by. How Mark had enjoyed the company of the fishermen there. "Grass roots chaps," he had called them, relishing their daily struggle with the reality of the elements when he had to contend with rush hours and business deadlines.

Abbie walked down the slipway and kept her mental promise to Chris to paddle whatever the weather. She tucked her socks in the pocket of her raincoat and rolled up her jeans and let the tamed water of the harbour creep inexorably around her ankles. Her eyes watered. It was unbelievably cold for August.

She walked barefoot into Mrs Enys' general store, already feeling she was calling on a friend. The white-haired lady was pleased to see her and appalled at her bare wet feet.

"Come through to my parlour, Mrs Eliot, do," she insisted, lifting the counter flap. "My goodness, you're as daft as my crazy family—paddling in this weather."

Abbie went obediently through into a charmingly cluttered and old-fashioned room and let herself be dried and coddled while she enquired about paint and materials and maybe a reasonable second-hand shop for a mirror. Mrs Enys entered thoroughly into the spirit of the thing.

"I stock paint, of course—oh yes, I'm not called a general store for nothing. But whether you'd get what you want from the haberdashers. . . ."

"Net curtaining would do," Abbie explained. "I can gather it thickly and it will look like something from Swan Lake. Very feminine."

Mrs Enys chuckled. "Hard to imagine anything in Margo Ritchie's cottage being feminine. One of her portraits is just a pile of bones, and when I mentioned it didn't look much like the sitter, she informed me it was the real person without any trimmings!"

Abbie said soberly, "I know what she means though. People put up such barrages of façades that sometimes you seem to see just . . . well, bare bones."

Mrs Enys said, "You might well understand Margo." She sighed. "She has great difficulty in . . . being understood. It's a pity you can't stay after the Bank Holiday."

"Oh, I am," Abbie said, relief that she could at last partially explain her presence here. "I'm teaching at the school. Daniel simply wouldn't give me chance to tell him—"

Mrs Enys smiled, also relieved. "He told me I mustn't ask you a thing, or bother you in any way—as if I would. He wants you to feel completely unfettered. You were kind to him before—"

"The children got on . . ." Abbie murmured, unwilling to go further. Daniel was right, emotional scenes got you nowhere.

Mrs Enys talked diffidently about the twins. "You'll have a handful there I'm afraid, Mrs Eliot," she confided, her smile now contrasting strongly with the worried look in her eyes. "I'm afraid Daniel shuts himself off from people sometimes." She looked down at her worn hands. "He won't even take any guests at the inn. Grief takes people in different ways and instead of bringing him closer to his children it frequently seems to drive him away."

Could that have happened with Chris if he had been spared? Abbie could not imagine it.

"I sold up last year and bought this store—didn't say a word to Daniel. But so far I've been too busy to help him much. I'm hoping when the winter comes—"

"Couldn't you have moved into the inn?" Abbie asked, curiosity overcoming reticence. "He probably needs help there to get it going."

"He won't hear of it. He's got a cook and a succession of cleaners and helpers. But he should take control." Mrs Enys looked helplessly at Abbie. "What can you do?"

Abbie frowned. Grief was a lonely business, but Daniel seemed to hug his loneliness to him when there was no need. He still had his boys . . . and his mother.

In the end she bought six yards of curtain net and a mirror from a rather expensive bric-a-brac shop. Mrs Enys packed the paint and a loaf of bread, half a pound of butter, cheese and assorted tins into a big plastic carrier. It was heavy and the rain hadn't stopped so the path was even slipperier. Abbie was exhausted as she trudged across the field in the middle of the afternoon.

Daniel was waiting at the kitchen door, obviously worried.

"Where on earth have you been?" he said irritably, relieving her of the mirror and the parcel of curtaining. "I've opened a tin of soup and put fish paste on some of those stale water biscuits—sit down—" He pushed her into the armchair and stuck her feet on a box in front of the dead fire. "You're absolutely soaked. I know you want to be alone, but what good will it do to make yourself ill?"

She smiled and then couldn't stop. She watched him re-light the fire with hands smeared with Gold Sunset. He had good hands, very broad and rather short-fingered. Mark had liked to watch him baiting fish hooks and pulling a boat ashore. He looked so much older; the beard did not suit him and had obviously grown because he could not be bothered to shave.

He brought in the meal he had prepared. The soup had a thick skin over its surface and the biscuits were crumbling under the weight of the fish paste, but Abbie hadn't enjoyed food so much for a long time.

"I paddled," she told him through a delicious mouthful. "Oh, this is lovely—how kind you are—and then I dried off at your mother's and bought some stuff for the bedroom and rummaged around an antique shop for the mirror—"

"You must have spent a fortune," he grumbled, eyeing her tumbled purchases without favour. "You'd better work out how much the bedroom stuff cost—"

She said, "Don't be silly, Daniel. I've got plenty of money—that's one thing I have got." The house had fetched an enormous price and then there had been the ghastly insurance.

He said nothing. She drank her soup appreciatively and after a while he got up and fetched more logs for the fire and then stood indecisively looking into the heart of the flames. He shook his head when she offered him a biscuit.

"I've eaten already," he told her. "And Tammy will be starting dinner soon. We have it early." So Tammy was the cook Mrs Enys had mentioned. He had been with Daniel before, a ship's cook who could turn his hand to anything. She was thankful he was still there, at least Daniel and the boys ate well and had warm, comfortable beds. "I ought to go. Will you be all right?"

"Of course. I'm going to paint the tea chest first so that it'll be dry enough to wear its skirt tomorrow. Could you get something to make a lid for it?"

He nodded almost absently. "Abbie—" he laid his arm along the mantelpiece and rested his head on it. "Forgive me, I know I said no questions or explanations, and I meant it. But—this trip to Linstowel—are you running away?"

She looked at him again, studied the dark depths of his face. Grief came in many ways, but there was a common denominator. . . .

"Yes. I suppose I am."

He straightened suddenly and walked to the window. He said almost mockingly, "I've tried it. It doesn't work."

"Perhaps—perhaps you went in the wrong direction."

He laughed shortly. "Perhaps. Sorry, Abbie, I'm no good at these word games." Restlessly he crossed to the kitchen door. "I don't work over the weekend. I spend my time with the boys and give my mother a hand in the shop. I'll try not to disturb you when I arrive on Monday."

He was gone. Suddenly and without even a goodnight, he had gone through the kitchen leaving the back door open to the drifting summer rain. It was a deliberate rebuff and Abbie felt stunned with the shock of it. She went over their conversation and could find no reason for his sudden departure. Of course, she hadn't known him very well two years ago and maybe his grief at the loss of his young wife then had masked the real person. Yet she had felt him a friend; a special person in a world of strangers—even then in the midst of her own happiness. And yesterday when he had come into the shop and she had seen him properly, it had been with a shock of recognition; that he was still someone special in a world of strangers.

Somehow she got through the rest of that day, forcing herself to sandpaper the tea chest and paint it, then carrying on with the chair and sitting up late gathering the nylon net into a crinoline petticoat. She was used to not letting herself think, but it got no easier.

On Saturday she could find no energy to do anything after a sleepless night, not even walk to Mrs Enys' shop for her weekend supplies. Nobody came near the cottage and a heavy mist joined the sea to land and sky. By tea-time Abbie was wondering half seriously whether she could be the only person left alive in the world. She had no television or wireless to connect her with the outside world, there were a few out-of-date newspapers on the floor in the second bedroom and she had some text-books in her case. She could have started to plan next term's work, or given the chair a top coat of paint, or even sanded down the frame of the mirror. Yet she did nothing. She felt as if she existed in a void.

The thought of the long evening, then the night, then half of tomorrow before she could move into the school house was too much. At half-past seven she remembered the social evening to be held in the church hall. With enormous relief she realised it was the sort of thing the new village schoolmistress should attend. It would please Lady Margaret and Mr Odgers even if Lampton and Mr Dawes might consider it frivolous.

Before she could have second thoughts, she went into the tiny bedroom off the sitting-room and changed into a blue dress. Her hair had dried fluffily and she pinned it severely behind her ears and used no make-up at all. She pulled her brogues over her tights and tucked some lighter shoes into her coat pocket. It was already growing dark but she had no torch so she left the kitchen light on as a guide for later on. The mist was like a fine rain on her face; she should have gone for a walk earlier, it would have done her good.

The little church hall was packed with people, holiday-makers instantly recognisable by their flowery dresses and open-necked shirts—it must be a boon for them to have somewhere to go this weather. Abbie saw quite a few vaguely familiar faces from two years ago and the Reverend Odgers raised a welcoming hand as he went round with raffle tickets. Abbie bought a cup of coffee and settled herself in a corner to watch a game with balloons. It was friendly and pleasant, people spoke to her, mostly complaining about the weather, but other, local people, who must have heard about her from Mrs Enys or the school managers, came up and enquired whether she was the new teacher and hoped she would be happy in Linstowel. She danced sedately with Mr Odgers, who introduced her to his wife and Mrs Dawes. Mrs Odgers was plump and made very little impression, but Mrs Dawes was a tiny, small-boned woman who sat by Abbie and "put her in the picture" with the local people in a warm way that contrasted oddly with what Abbie remembered of her husband's dry manner. She confided that Mr Dawes had stayed at home because "he likes conversation, not chit-chat". Abbie laughed. She could imagine Mr Dawes' gentle insistence on staying by his own fireside.

The evening was coming to a gradual end with a last waltz when there was a flurry at the doorway and Daniel appeared. He had obviously come from the inn without a coat, and his jersey, like his hair and beard, was beaded with the fine rain. He stood with his hands in his pockets, gazing around the hall broodingly, out of place in the genteel atmosphere.

"Now this could be trouble, my dear," Mrs Dawes said in her ear. "Mr Enys is a man for whom extreme grief means anger with the whole world. Something has upset him. Probably his two small boys—they're both at your school incidentally. The sight of our rather narrow pleasure will infuriate him."

Abbie turned from the sight of Daniel's unhappy figure.

"I think I'll go then," she said to Mrs Dawes. "I do know Mr Enys, in fact I am using the cottage belonging to his friend Miss Ritchie. I would rather not see anything . . . upsetting."

"I quite understand, my child—"

But even as Mrs Dawes began her farewells, Daniel was at their sides. He held Abbie's arm again and this time his grip was not reassuring.

"Mrs Eliot I believe," he said in a voice that came close to a sneer. "Our new school marm—"

Abbie tried to pull away. "I must go now, Daniel. Excuse me—"

"Would you refuse me the last dance?" He was already pulling her on to the floor while Mrs Dawes watched with blue eyes wide.

"Daniel. What's the matter? Stop it—please—people will misunderstand—"

"And that mustn't happen, must it? You've got a position to keep up—" He whirled her giddily under the paper lanterns and she clung to him, feeling sick at the almost physical impact of his anger. "No wonder you want the twins to stay on in Linstowel school, my dear. Two more off the register and you might have to close, mightn't you? Then no job for little Abbie who is running away from the only happiness worth having—"

"You've been drinking," she almost sobbed. "Please stop by the cloakroom. I must go."

He held her savagely, forcing her to listen.

"I know what it is to want to get away—I thought, by giving you the cottage for the weekend, I could be saving a marriage I'd always admired. A perfect marriage." He gave a reckless laugh. "When my mother told me you were the new school marm—that your escape was a permanent one—I couldn't believe it. You fool, Abbie—you crazy fool—"

She was crying now as she had known she would when it came to the moment of truth. "Daniel, she—you—only know half the story. Mark and Chris were killed in a car accident a year ago last February—now let me go—"

Somehow she was into the cloakroom and had her coat and heavy shoes bundled under one arm. When she emerged she saw Daniel sitting next to Mrs Dawes and then she was through the door and outside in the darkness and rain.

She was halfway up the cliff path when she heard him shout behind her.

"Abbie! Wait—I've got a torch—wait for me!"

She tried to run but her sandals were against her in the muddy lane and Daniel's outstretched hand caught her arm before she had even reached the field.

She held herself rigidly away from him, tears still running down her face. Beneath them the sea pounded.

"Abbie, I didn't know—you realise that."

"It's all right. It's not you. I always break down when

I tell people. You were right before, it does no good to talk about it."

There was a silence while they stood in the darkness recovering. His grip on her arm did not slacken; it hurt because—somehow it was still angry.

At last he said, "Come on. Let me see you home." He produced a torch from his pocket and they stumbled on through the five-barred gate and across the field to where the kitchen light was like a beacon in the rain-filled darkness.

She began immediately to make coffee; there was comfort in the small everyday tasks. The fire had long gone out and they sat in the chilly living-room, the uncurtained window a black square. Again, there seemed nothing to say.

At last she spoke, her voice high and formal. "You didn't give me a chance to tell you yesterday. I move into the school house tomorrow afternoon, so I won't see you here again. Thank you for letting me use the cottage. The bedroom is almost finished. Just the mirror."

He said, "You're hating me because I haven't invested my grief with dignity as you have."

"No, of course not. Daniel, I'm tired. Please go."

"You're frightened of me—yes you are—" as she made to protest. "You can't understand me—neglecting my boys, my business, myself. You're just like the others. You've only been here two days and already you're getting the picture. The drunken orgies in this cottage —you'll have heard about Margo and me of course?"

"No—Daniel, please go—"

"Did you come back thinking we could pool our unhappiness, Abbie? Poor Abbie. What a shock it must have been to hear about Margo and me—" He began to laugh and she clapped her hands over her ears. He seized them angrily and dragged them down. "You don't know anything about the degradation of grief, do you, Abbie? You're earning your halo by getting on with life as best you can—" He mimicked Mr Odgers' voice cruelly. "And you came down here to take up the memory of your happy holiday—when you in your—innocence—your smug happiness—thought you were helping a widower and his orphaned brats—"

Her tears blinded her. "How can you speak like this, Daniel?"

"Because up to a point we're in the same boat, my dear. But you're not facing reality. You're building up a lovely picture of Abigail Eliot, dedicating her lonely life to others. Whereas I know that all grief does is to take beauty and dignity away, to degrade—"

She tried to push past him into the kitchen and found herself gripped in his arms. His face was close to hers, filling her whole world, and then his mouth crushed against her mouth in an embrace that was not a kiss. He lifted his head again and stared down at her for a long minute, then he stumbled through the kitchen and out into the night.

THREE

IF DANIEL had indeed wished to show Abbie some of
the degradation of his personal grief, he had more than
succeeded, and she spent a miserable night going over
the scene again and again, examining her own motives
in coming down here in the light of Daniel's bitter
remarks. Was she really as superficial as he thought?
Had she really thought to recapture any of the happiness
of that last holiday with her family, or even—the worst
of all—to rescue Daniel and settle down with him and
the twins? Her pride cried out against this and she
covered her face with her hands as if she could shut out
the sensation of Daniel's mouth on hers. He had said
he wanted to shake her, and that was exactly what he
had done. She was shaken to the very core of her being,
finally questioning the veracity of her grief.

With the grey of daylight she tried to adopt her
previous attitude to her continuing life. Somehow it had
to be lived however meaningless it had become, and the
immediate answer was to keep steadily busy. She tidied
up the cottage and left a note of thanks to Miss Ritchie.
Then she settled herself at the kitchen table with her
notebook and the register Miss Liddell had given her
last term after the interview.

By mid-day, after five hours' planning, she had

covered a vast amount of work and had recovered some of the calm self-control which she had known to impress Mr Dawes and Lady Margaret. Not only had she studied Miss Liddell's notes on the children and divided them into age groups and even re-arranged the seating plan on the rough sketch she had made of the school, but she had made a programme for herself, to cover the next three days until the children arrived on Thursday morning. She had other notes which she had made during the summer on more ambitious teaching plans, and these she assembled into some kind of order. She began to remember how it felt to be a teacher, to see the term ahead taking some sort of shape, to feel intense curiosity about the children she would work with, to want to roll up her sleeves and get cracking.

She made coffee and sandwiches for herself and walked down to the edge of the cliff while the coffee cooled. It was warmer than yesterday, still misty but with a definite conviction that above the mist was an August sun. On the other side of the cliff road there was a sloping reach of short grass ending in a tumble of giant rocks which seemed to hold the land from slipping down the cliff face to the sea below. The tide was far enough out for a tiny pebbled beach to be visible beyond the creaming surf and Abbie clambered down to it with some difficulty, letting the water fill her plimsolls and enjoying the salty discomfort of the wet canvas. She stood there in the suck and gurgle of the tide and said aloud to the uncaring sea, "I do not wish to see Daniel Enys ever again. And the sooner he sends his sons to boarding school the better for them. And for me." It was like a vow; the spoken words seemed to release her from some of the ugliness Daniel had forced her to see. She stretched her arms far above her head and could feel the warmth of the invisible sun. It would be all right. She would make it all right. There were a lot of difficulties which she had not foreseen when she arrived for the interview, but she would get to know the children and they would be her salvation.

A voice hailing her from above interrupted her thoughts. She went further into the sea to get a glimpse of the new arrival and saw Mr Dawes gesticulating with a bone-handled cane. He was in the same suit he had worn for the interview—of course it was Sunday today— but looked far from his calm self then.

He cupped his voice against the sound of the surf.

"Are you all right, Mrs Eliot?"

Abbie nodded vigorously.

"Do come up—it's not really safe—" He went on to say something about the tide, which Abbie could not hear.

Resignedly she began to climb back up, not enjoying the experience any more with wet, slippery shoes and an audience as well. His firm handgrip was more than welcome as she reached the big rocks bordering the cliff turf.

"Very dangerous, Mrs Eliot," he panted, putting a hand beneath her elbow and leading her to a natural seat in the granite. "The tide you know—" He was obviously trying to reconcile the linen-suited woman he had seen last June with this trousered figure in soaking plimsolls and pale hair lying damply against her neck. "It wouldn't do to begin term with a broken ankle!"

"Please don't worry, Mr Dawes. I've done some climbing before. And the tide isn't coming in. I noticed the times yesterday."

"My dear, an outgoing tide is just as dangerous here— if you had lost your footing you would have been swept out to sea very quickly."

She smiled at him, suddenly grateful for his concern. "I won't do it again, Mr Dawes," she promised like an erring pupil. "But it's done me so much good. The physical effort has evaporated a stupid mood."

He sat down just below her. "My wife told me of last night's unfortunate incident with Mr Enys. He seemed genuinely worried, however, when she acquainted him with the true facts. Apparently he was under the impression you had left your family, and it angered him."

"Yes. Yes, it angered him."

He looked up at her seriously. "I understand you met Mr Enys when you were here on holiday, Mrs Eliot, so you will know he lost his wife in peculiar circumstances. It changed him. Sometimes he is his old self, charming and helpful. Other times he is a strangely embittered man who will strike out at others as if he hates their very normalcy."

"I realise he is a victim of moods. I did not realise his wife died in—peculiar circumstances, however. But frankly, Mr Dawes, I would rather not talk about Mr Enys."

61

"My wife told me you were very upset and left the social immediately after Mr Enys approached you. I merely hoped to make the inexplicable . . . explicable."

"Thank you. I do appreciate that." Abbie stared over the respectable trilby which covered Mr Dawes' long head, wondering how many other people would find it necessary to explain Daniel. "It was an enjoyable evening—at the church hall. I was pleased to meet your wife . . ." Her voice trailed away. She wondered whether Mr Dawes was going to disturb her carefully fostered composure.

"She was delighted to meet you, Mrs Eliot. That is why I am here. She understands you are moving into the school house this afternoon and wondered whether you would lunch with us. I have come straight from church —my car is on the road—and I can transport you and your luggage first to our little bungalow and then on to the school house."

"Mr Dawes, you are both so kind—" Abbie felt unexpected tears of gratitude in her eyes, though her immediate reaction was to decline the invitation. "I really do appreciate—but I couldn't burst in on your quiet Sunday lunch. I've made coffee and sandwiches— they're waiting for me at the cottage—and I really feel I am not good company today."

"Mrs Eliot"—the piercing grey eyes were very understanding; he must have been a good headmaster—"that is the very time you need company." He smiled suddenly. "It is such a sensible arrangement anyway, my child. How will you get your case down the cliff road and then up the combe—you will be exhausted before you begin. And while I am happy to come and fetch you later on, it would be pleasanter altogether if you would allow me to help you now. After all, I am here."

Put like that it would be churlish to refuse, and Abbie had not even considered the physical difficulties of humping her luggage. They walked slowly across the field to the cottage while Mr Dawes told her about the surface tin that the old miner who first built the cottage had grubbed from the cliff face over a hundred years ago.

"He made quite a decent living at it and his son continued to do so, building the lean-to kitchen on to the cottage and then the second bedroom when his family expanded. Unfortunately he fell to his death during a gale and *his* son found that the small surface seam was exhausted, so the cottage was sold to Mr Lampton's grandfather for fifty guineas and his shepherd lived there till the present Lampton let it for a holiday cottage."

"It doesn't belong to Miss Ritchie?" Abbie asked as she led the way inside and seated her guest while she threw away her coffee and washed the mug, then wrapped her sandwiches for a possible evening snack.

"No." Mr Dawes lost some of his teacher's manner. "Lampton sold it to Ghislaine Enys. She used it as a studio. I believe her friend Miss Ritchie leases it from Enys."

Abbie clattered the crockery as she stacked it neatly in its cupboard. All roads in Linstowel seemed to lead back to the Enys family. She had never heard Daniel's wife's name mentioned before. Ghislaine. A name that made the dead woman seem suddenly real to Abbie who had never seen her. A painter. And her friend now used her cottage for painting, too.

"I'll go and change and then I shall be ready, Mr Dawes. I'm sorry to keep you waiting."

"Not at all, Mrs Eliot. We always have a late Sunday lunch in any case." He stood up tactfully. "I will leave you to lock up and take some of your luggage down to the car."

"Thank you." She watched him for a moment as he carried her heavy case across the field. He was an upright man, but not unbending. She had a sudden feeling she would need friends like Mr and Mrs Dawes.

Lunch was a pleasant, homely occasion. Mrs Dawes had roasted a chicken which she assured Abbie had had a happy life "trotting around like chickens do, my dear, not all cooped up in one of those battery things", and there was home-made apple tart. "We had a good crop this year, Mrs Eliot," boasted Mr Dawes, pointing out a luxuriant apple tree in need of drastic pruning. Then coffee in the tiny lounge overlooking the cliffs while the Dawes explained their riotous garden. "My wife cannot bear to uproot one tiny weed," Mr Dawes accused, looking at her fondly. "And my husband does not allow me to pick one flower," Mrs Dawes counter-attacked, standing in front of the jar of flop-headed dahlias in the empty grate.

When Mr Dawes had gone to pack a box with cooking

apples and vegetables, "just to start your week's menu, Mrs Eliot," Mrs Dawes took the chance of confiding to Abbie, "It will be lovely for Arnold to have you at the school, my dear. I've noticed he can talk to you. He never could to Miss Liddell. And the person before that had been here when the school opened."

Abbie flushed with pleasure. "I didn't realise how much I needed the sort of pampering I've had from you today."

Perhaps she was even more delighted when in the privacy of the car, Mr Dawes confided, "I am delighted with your appointment for personal reasons as well as community ones, Mrs Eliot. It will be delightful for my wife to have the kind of woman she can talk to. She occasionally sees Mrs Odgers and Lady Margaret, and of course she is on friendly terms with most of the women in the village, but I have noticed how easy she feels with you."

That was a compliment indeed. To be accepted as a teacher was one thing, but to be accepted as a human being was surely a sign that she might be recovering in spite of everything.

"Thank you, Mr Dawes. Believe me, I shall appreciate your wife's company whenever she can spare an evening to come to the school house . . ." She got out of the car. "No, please don't come inside. You've done such a lot for me I would feel much happier if you returned home now." She glanced up at the cottage. "Obviously Miss Liddell has gone so I can take my time and settle in gradually." She found the key in her pocket and followed

Mr Dawes up the steps to the front porch. He put her case carefully to one side of the door.

"Are you certain—? I am afraid Lampton hasn't got around to the painting and you will find a lot to be done besides that. I hardly like to leave you—"

She convinced him at last and stood in the porch until he drove on up the combe. Then with a sense of something beginning—until then she had only been conscious of things finishing—she unlocked the door and opened it on to the vestibule and stairs, with the sitting-room door wide at one side revealing her enormous trunk blocking the way to the kitchen. To the side of the trunk was a box which she recognised as containing her books, and on the other side a wicker basket in which she had carefully packed photographs and pictures. Luckily the few pieces of furniture she had kept would not be arriving until next week. She had plenty to get on with.

She spent the next hour investigating her new domain. Miss Liddell had left everything scrupulously clean, there was clean paper in all the drawers, the cutlery had obviously been polished, the stone bread crock well scoured and, in spite of the old-fashioned furniture and out-of-date equipment, everything sparkled and looked welcoming. Miss Liddell had also left a long memorandum which required some sorting out; postal times and milk and bread deliveries were interspersed with remarks like, "Janie Thompson—hole-in-heart—special P.E." . . . "Carpet in sitting-room shampooed three weeks ago" . . . and "original curtains in blanket box if required". It ended up, "The best of luck, you'll need it," and added a telephone number in Casterbridge "for emergencies".

Abbie looked at the curtains and decided to use her own although they would all be too long for the Victorian sash windows. The plain green of her curtains would be a quiet background to the overcrowded study and sitting-room, and upstairs she would like to open her eyes in the morning to her own bedroom curtains of garlanded roses. By the time she had hung them, it was almost dark, and she boiled a kettle for tea while she put her books in the bookcases and hung her favourite pictures.

She considered starting on the trunk, but decided against it and settled down with a cup of tea to write name cards for the children's coat pegs. She consulted her register and saw that she had four children rising five, who had come for a few days last term to get used to school. Smiling to herself, she began to draw outline figures beneath their names. What would Alison Wyatt look like, how could she best identify herself and her peg? Abbie drew her with a skipping rope and dancing pigtails. Miles Filbert and Stephen Tanner both had footballs, and she drew them so that when the cards were mounted they would be kicking their balls towards each other. Janie Thompson stood straight beside a hoop that was nearly as big as herself. Finally Abbie covered all seventeen name cards with clear plastic and stacked them in a box. It occured to her as she did so that the seventeen children at Linstowel school came from just ten families. No wonder County Hall wanted to close the school.

It had been a busy day and she was tired. She was washing her tea-cup and still discovering crockery and glass when there was a peremptory knock at the front door. She froze where she was. It was horrifying—somehow shaming—to discover that Daniel had been so near her conscious thoughts all day that she assumed her first visitor to the cottage must be he. Yet who else could it be? It was not the knock Mr Dawes would give and no one else knew she had moved in.

She looked in the old-fashioned mirror above the mantelpiece in the sitting-room. Her hair was messy and she tidied it with hands she saw were trembling. Thank goodness she had changed into a dress for her lunch with the Dawes'. It was somehow imperative that she appear before Daniel as the head mistress of Linstowel school, and not the vulnerable, rain-soaked woman of the night before.

She switched on the light in the tiny vestibule and opened the door. It was at once a relief and a terrible disappointment to find Lampton standing in the porch. The three months since she had seen him before had burnt his face to a brick red and his brown hair had bleached to a gingery crop. He poked his head just as aggressively, however, and his hooked Punch nose seemed to quest about for possible intruders before he grunted acknowledgement to her immediate invitation and edged past her into the sitting-room.

"Just arrived, I see," he said, eyeing the burly trunk.

"Yes." She saw no point in explaining about her arrival last Thursday and the awful hiatus of her stay in

Margo Ritchie's cottage. "Would you care for a sherry, Mr Lampton? Or some coffee?"

"No time for socialities—" she smiled at the coined word, but he stared back at her from his pale blue eyes and made his point—"Some of us have got work to do, Mrs Eliot."

She remembered the phrase from the interview and said sweetly, "Yes, but I don't mind pausing a few minutes," as she settled herself in an armchair with a gracious air.

He looked almost pleased at this retort and condescended to sit on the edge of a hard chair as he said in congratulation, "Reckon you'll be a match for County Hall. They're sure to turn up early, either next week or week after in the hopes of catching us out."

Abbie tried to sound amused. "Inspectors aren't even called that now, Mr Lampton. They're called Advisers. And that's what they do. Their job is not to catch anyone out. It is to help a school reach its full potential."

"Words. Words, which boil down to the same thing," Lampton said contemptuously. "They want to close us down, and we've got to keep one jump ahead of them."

"Yes, well, let's have one thing clear, please." Abbie was smarting under his brusque speech and manner. "I will run this school as economically as it is possible to run a school and I will not resort to the usual channels when something is needed—until I have consulted the managers. But if I consider that just one child is losing out on such a shoe-string system, I shall not hesitate to inform County Hall of my opinion."

There was a silence while Lampton's brick-red face deepened colour to puce. Then he stuttered, "I thought you were on our side!"

"Maybe I am, if your side is the same side as the children's. It would appear that in all the local feelings you mention, their well-being has somehow been overlooked. You have a child at this school yourself, Mr Lampton. Surely you want the best for her, even if she has to pay the price of leaving the village for seven hours of her day?"

"I'm a bachelor, Mrs Eliot. Rita is my brother's girl, and of course I take her well-being into consideration. That's why I want the local school kept on. You know all this. We went into it at the interview."

"I haven't forgotten. I wondered if you had. Sometimes the battle can become so exciting one loses sight of its aims."

Again he said nothing, but she could hear him breathing heavily. At last he grunted, "You're a good one with the words. I'll give you that. If you can spin them the same way for the Inspector, you'll do all right."

Abbie said wearily, "We seem to be back where we started. Did you have anything special to tell me, Mr Lampton? I'm very tired."

"I heard you had a late night last night," he said grimly.

She sat up straight. So he had known all the time that she had been in Linstowel since Thursday. He might look like a laughable Punch-figure, but he was more like a cunning old fox. He stood up and shoved his chair against the old mahogany sideboard.

"I came to tell you I can spare a man from the hay-making tomorrow to start painting the kitchen or bath-room. Which would be most convenient?"

She almost clucked with annoyance. She had wanted tomorrow to unpack her trunk and be quite by herself, and he had had all the summer holiday, after all. . . .

"The bathroom, I suppose," she said ungratefully. "He can have that to himself. I shall be very busy in the kitchen. Perhaps it would be better to postpone that until half-term."

"Well, the Inspector will look at the kitchen if you go on with that idea for letting the kiddies cook there—"

"Oh, well, the kitchen then. And that reminds me. You mentioned something about the blacksmith repairing the school stove—"

"We have to wait his convenience—"

"When he comes, could he sharpen the carpentry tools? I noticed the saw and balsa wood knife were practically useless."

"Naturally. We don't want the kiddies to cut them-selves, do we?"

She almost snapped his head off. "Neither do we want them to go mad with frustration, Mr Lampton. I am employed to show them how to use tools properly and to stop them carving each other up."

He held up a conciliatory hand. "All right, Mrs Eliot —every man to his own job. I'll ask my man to bring them back with him tomorrow. I've got an oilstone at

my place and can do them before school starts." He
went towards the door and stood with his hand on the
knob and his back to Abbie. "Mrs Eliot . . . you will find
that if there is anything practical to be done about the
cottage or school . . . I am usually the one to do it. So
I wish . . ."

Abbie stood up quickly. She realised how hard it was
for a man like Lampton to hold out a hand of friendship
and she was touched by his change of tone.

"I would prefer you as an ally anyway, Mr Lampton,"
she said with a smile in her voice.

He went through into the vestibule and again paused,
darting her a glance over his shoulder. She noticed his
old Harris tweed jacket was patterned with straw here
and there and it made him somehow endearing.

"Then you won't mind me saying—no, warning you
against Daniel Enys. If you've come down here hoping
to resume his acquaintanceship—don't. Enys is a dis-
reputable character and for the good of the school it
would be much better if you saw as little of him as
possible."

Abbie said sharply, "Don't say any more, Mr Lampton, please. I have no intention of having anything to
do with Mr Enys. But what I do with my private life
is my own concern."

He straightened himself and his pale eyes were on a
level with her own. "You know that isn't so, Mrs Eliot.
Not entirely. Not as school mistress of this school."

The truth of this forced her to silence. They stared at
each other, breathing fast. Abbie felt herself on a see-saw,

one moment respecting, almost liking this blunt, practical man, the next resenting him fiercely.

He went on pleadingly, "His wife used to paint in that cottage, Mrs Eliot—she had to get away by herself, and she used to spend hours there, painting and reading. Now that Ritchie woman turns up for a week or two and they—they have orgies!"

It sounded naïve, almost pathetic. She wanted to laugh in his face.

"Please go, Mr Lampton. I don't want to hear any gossip—" She almost pushed him physically from the house.

The weathered face darkened with anger. "All right, I'll go. But if I'm to be an ally, Mrs Eliot, like you said, then you must heed my warning. Everyone knows there was a scene at the church hall last night between you and Enys. Don't let the gossip grow. It will if you're not careful—this is a small village." He opened the door and stepped out into the darkness. Cloud hid the moon as it had hidden the sun and he disappeared before he had taken two of the steps to the combe lane. She slammed the door on him and stood against it with her eyes tight shut. Was she never to have a peaceful night in Linstowel?

After a while she went automatically into the kitchen and put the kettle on, though she didn't really want another drink. There would be no sleep for her if she couldn't calm herself before she went to bed. Then she realised with irritation that she could not in fact make up her bed until she had unpacked the linen from the trunk.

By the time she had found the keys and unlocked and unstrapped Mark's old trunk, the kettle had boiled for coffee. And then she made up the bed and put out her travelling alarm and a glass of water and a book. It wasn't until she drank her coffee that she realised Lampton's malevolence against Daniel had had an opposite effect from the one he intended. Unexpectedly she felt a new sympathy for Daniel struggling against such searching village gossip. Yet, at the same time, she cringed at the implication that she was now part of that gossip; Linstowel would probably think, with Lampton, that she had come down here to meet Daniel again. She sighed and pressed the palms of her hands against her forehead. How much easier things would be if Daniel removed his boys from the school—if he left the village altogether.

She sighed again and stood up to go upstairs and the telephone rang.

This time intuition was right.

'Abbie?" Daniel's voice was hesitant. "Don't put the phone down. I'm not going to talk. I just . . . are you all right, Abbie? I mean, is the cottage comfortable? And—are you all right?"

She paused, wondering what on earth to say.

At last she said, "I'm weary, Daniel. I can't think straight. All I know is I don't want to see or hear from you again."

Gently she replaced the receiver. She found she was weeping.

FOUR

To ABBIE'S surprise she slept like a log and spent a curious Bank Holiday coping with the friendly farm worker who came to paint her kitchen. She tried to produce at least one reasonable meal from the iron rations she had with her; the dairy was the only shop open—and that only for an hour during the morning—so she bought more cheese and milk, butter and eggs and squeezed around the paint pots and ladder to make a passable omelette which Mr Lampton's man ate in three mouthfuls. The following day she went to Mrs Enys' shop and stocked up properly and then spent the afternoon in the dusty old school while a top coat of paint was put on in the kitchen.

The school cleaner had been busy all morning washing paintwork, and Abbie worked with her, scrubbing tables and chairs and then the floor. After tea, in the last two hours of the late summer daylight, they cleaned the windows and washed the lamp shades.

"It looks lovely, doesn't it, miss?" said Mrs Thompson, who had two children at the school. "Some of them in the village, they say it's a second-rate building with second-rate staff—begging your pardon, miss—I know you'll make them change their minds about that right off." Abbie smiled. If only she could. It would somehow vindicate her decision to come here. Wipe away the smear that her old friendship with Daniel had become. "But what I say is—" went on Mrs Thompson, who was proving indefatigable in more ways than one—"they might not have posh books and the piano might be a bit out of tune, but there's nothing second rate about that building. Good solid stone, and Mr Lampton's kept it up a treat with this nice cream paint—"

"It certainly does look attractive," Abbie murmured, looking around with pleasure as the evening sun turned the old yellow wood floor to gold. "I wonder if Mr Lampton could arrange for some book shelves just here. I noticed Miss Liddell had a few books on a table, but it doesn't show them off to their best—"

"Well, miss, the books are very old, you see. The mothers mostly bring them in from home. And Miss Liddell keeps the readers in her own desk in case they gets torn."

"Doesn't the library van call once a month?"

"Oh, no. We don't get nothing down from Caster-bridge. Mr Lampton should've told you."

"Yes, he did, Mrs Thompson," Abbie said quickly.

The tough little woman rolled up her overall and put it in a shapeless bag. "That's what I mean. None of the latest things like at Castle Combe. But, like I said, it's only just down the road and that makes a difference when you've got a little one like my Janie."

"Oh, yes." Abbie suddenly remembered Miss Liddell's

note. "Of course, your daughter has a heart condition. You filled in the form, did you, Mrs Thompson?"

"Oh, yes. And told Miss Liddell all about it. And Lady Margaret. Cos she comes into school sometimes and I wanted her to keep an eye on Janie for me—" Abbie realised with an inward smile that Lady Margaret had doubtless been asked to keep an eye on the new teacher as well. Mrs Thompson went into long clinical details and Abbie edged towards the door.

"Do I see you in the mornings, Mrs Thompson?" she prompted as she tested the lights one by one.

"Oh, yes, miss. I pop over about eight and get the stove going in the winter, or open up the windows. Generally air the place out you know. Then I arrive about half-past three, as soon as I've got Janie home to her gran, and clean up for a couple of hours. It was longer for Miss Liddell, of course—being young. She used to have paint all over the place, and if they'd used any glue—" She made sounds of despair.

Abbie couldn't help laughing at Mrs Thompson's brutal honesty. "Let's hope I don't find you too much to do. I believe in children clearing up their own muddles, so I hope we shan't keep you after five o'clock this term." Privately she thought as there were only half-a-dozen toilets and wash basins, Mrs Thompson should get through her work in an hour easily. "I shall probably work until then myself, unless I find it more convenient to come back later in the evening."

She locked the door carefully and waved goodbye to Mrs Thompson. She felt a clutch of nerves in her stomach at the thought of those children arriving the day after tomorrow. All with their individual problems and little ways.

Wednesday flew by. It was early closing in Linstowel and Mrs Enys arrived during the afternoon to find Abbie arranging flowers and mounting displays.

"You haven't stopped for lunch!" Daniel's mother accused. "I could see you were the conscientious sort when you plunged into that decorating up at Margo's cottage. I wanted Daniel to come and give you a hand, or send the boys, but he said it wouldn't do—whatever that might mean."

"He was right," Abbie said diplomatically. "So are you—I had no idea it was so late. I'll just run down to the dairy and get some cottage cheese—"

"It's early closing," said Mrs Enys, spreading a clean tea towel over one of the little tables. "And I always have a sandwich anyway, so I thought, why not have it with Mrs Eliot—"

"Please call me Abbie, it would make me feel so much more at home." Abbie eyed the growing feast appearing on the tea towel and started to laugh. "Honestly, anyone would think I was starving."

"My dear child, you'll have to look after yourself properly. I had the same difficulty when I came here this year—overwork. But at least I had food all around me in the shop. I understand you've no refrigerator." She settled herself in a tiny chair and poured coffee from a giant thermos. "Now why don't you get one? You could have it on hire purchase if the outlay was a bit much. Then you'd be able to get enough food on a Saturday to last most of the week. You can have bread and milk delivered, and Mr Thompson will bring you in fresh vegetables . . ." She chatted on, organising Abbie's domestic life for her, making it easy to sit down and help herself to the delicious chicken sandwiches and firm tomatoes. How odd it was that she got on so well with Daniel's mother, yet Daniel sparked off instant animosity.

She enjoyed taking Mrs Enys around and explaining her layout. She had used one of the bookcases from the house to screen off an angle for a book corner, and the carpet had arrived this morning with her other personal things from home, so she had laid and tacked it down carefully and put two or three cushions down, hoping children would be encouraged to sit and browse through a selection of her own books from the wicker basket. Of course, they weren't enough, she told Mrs Enys eagerly; they would have to order information books and big picture books from the County Library, but it was a beginning.

Just outside the book corner was a colour display. She had chosen yellow, which would fit in with the early autumn leaves, and had draped bright yellow material from the high window to the ground and pinned on a few yellow articles—a colander, a ribbon, a plastic spoon. She would soon have yellow pictures from the children to add to these.

There was a word-table, too. Pictures of houses, cardboard models of people and dogs, all carefully labelled.

A string of big letter cards hung along one side of the room and a number strip the other. There was a nature table, only just started, with sea shells from the beach, which would be continued by the children, and an interest table for the older ones with a small microscope and hand lenses. And there were flowers everywhere, dahlias and roses and spiky lavender and enormous sunflowers. All she needed was children.

They came in force the next day, arriving soon after eight-thirty while she was still putting out thread and beads for her younger ones and mixing paint for the ten-year-olds. They brought quite a few curious mums with them, too, who hung around and claimed her attention when she should have been introducing herself to the children. But she knew the importance of establishing good relationships with parents and smiled as she listened to details of summer colds and the necessity for coats at playtime. After the grey weekend the sun had decided to shine and it promised to be a warm day.

"Let me show Miles and Stephen their pegs . . ." She led anxious mothers and eager little boys into the narrow stone-floored cloakroom which she had brightened with a poster about washing hands and cleaning teeth. They were delighted with their football pictures and hung their new caps and blazers solemnly in place. Mrs Thompson's ten-year-old, Marilyn, a small girl like her mother, with thick brown plaits and a ready smile, was helping her sister to hang her outdoor things on the peg decorated with the picture of the girl and hoop. She told Abbie her name and added, "Mum says I got to help our Janie to put on her daps and all—" She glanced in the direction of the toilets. Abbie nodded. Janie Thompson would have to learn that she was not a helpless invalid, but it would be a gradual process.

The arrival of the Enys twins caused a near uproar. Most of the children had come into the school immediately they arrived to see the new teacher, and had stayed to examine her innovations, so the playground was quiet and empty except for departing mothers. Paul and Peter elected to run around the school making a roaring noise which frightened the new ones and made Mrs Thompson clutch Janie against her overall. Luckily a familiar face appeared in the doorway grinning a welcome, and Abbie put an immediate name to it.

"Stanley Berrows? I remember you from last term— would you fetch the school bell and ring it in the playground please. It's practically nine o'clock."

He jumped to it eagerly, and by the time he had finished a prolonged tolling, Paul and Peter had run out of breath. Abbie, standing quietly at her desk, could hear Stan's rather hectoring instructions to "find your name in the cloakroom double-quick—you can't have any old peg like last time." She hadn't intended making everything difficult and different for the children and wondered momentarily whether it would prove too much for them. Then, looking at the small faces turned towards her, bright with anticipation, she knew she had been right to transform the school as she had done. Already there was trust in those young expressions. In the brief exploration and consultations they had held

81

while she dealt with the new ones, it was as if they had decided she knew what she was about and they could safely put themselves in her hands.

She didn't risk the familiarity of a smile just yet. The four new children holding her hand were trying to tell her where they had been sitting before she changed everything around. She whispered to them that she would find them a place in a moment. Then she waited quietly for Paul and Peter to come into the classroom.

Paul came in first, jauntily, cockily, probably because he had heard from his father or grandmother that he knew Mrs Eliot. Peter followed more slowly—Abbie decided immediately that Peter was not always Paul's willing follower. They both looked surprised at the still classroom.

"What's up?" queried Paul loudly. "Tied knots in your tongues?"

Several girls snickered and Abbie said softly, "Sit anywhere for now, boys, while I take the register."

Paul cupped his ear. "Eh?" he quavered in an old man's voice, "I didn't quite catch—"

"Sit down!" Abbie rapped, and felt Jane Thompson's hand jump in hers. She had the satisfaction of seeing the boys drop like stones into the nearest seats. She gently helped the little ones to sit at a table near her desk and then said, "Good morning, children—" then before they could wonder how to reply, she went on quickly, "My name is Mrs Eliot and I am your new teacher. The school will be open every morning if you would prefer to come inside instead of playing in the play-

ground. You are welcome to use the reading corner or
interest tables at any time, but when the bell rings you
will sit still and be quite quiet while I call the register
and collect the dinner money. Then we shall discuss our
work and I will give you jobs to do. Sometime between
ten and half past the little ones will have their milk and
then we shall have prayers—"

"Excuse me, Mrs Eliot." It was Rita Lampton being
very polite. "We always had prayers straight off."

"I prefer them later, Rita, but thank you for telling
me. Some of the little ones are tired when they arrive
and I would like them to think about what we say and
do in prayers."

Paul made a scraping noise with his chair and grinned
furtively around his table. Abbie ignored him and began
on the register. As she gathered in the dinner money the
scraping grew louder.

"Paul Enys," she said very quietly. But he heard this
time.

"Yes, miss—"

"Dinner money, Paul? Thank you. Now stay by my
desk please."

He looked defiant. "Why? I haven't done anything."

"I would like you to count the dinner money, please.
All the fifties in this box. Ten pences in this . . ."

She finished the registers and told them a few more
things—not too much to begin with. Then she chose her
helpers for the next few days; Paul Enys to fetch the
register and count dinner money on Monday, Marilyn
Thompson to keep an eye on the new ones—while she

was seeing to her sister she might as well see to the others
—Rita Lampton and Bob Wyatt to keep the flowers
fresh, Stan Berrows to ring the school bell, Lily and
Wesley Wyatt to change the date and weather chart each
day. There were other jobs which would crop up later
so that even the five-year-olds could have small positions
of responsibility.

Meanwhile she started on her morning story, no easy
task with such varying ages. First of all it had to be
interesting for all of them, then it had to be a starter
for some writing or craft work, and preferably something
that could be developed through other work. She had
brought with her a jam jar of earth containing a worm
which she called William. She held him limp over her
finger and let the little girls shudder aloud and the boys
boast about worms they had in their gardens, then she
began her tale of William Worm, the youngest in the
family, who was too shy to go to parties and had stayed
at home until he was—well, this size, and then decided
on a spurt of courage that he must leave home and find
his fortune. She recounted his farewells and promises to
Mother and Father Worm to be good and to do his best
and to try to stop being shy and live with other worms,
but immediately he left his family, he wriggled his way
to a lonely spot in a garden underneath an apple tree
and wouldn't speak to the other worms. If only he could
find someone or something to help him.

By ten o'clock she had handed over the big plastic
aquarium she had found in the attic of the school house
to her four top-group children and sent them off to her

garden armed with trowels to begin the wormery for William. The little ones were drawing the sort of house they thought William should have—which looked very like the one on the word table, and the others were industriously beginning "The Adventures of William Worm. Part one." All too soon she was organising the under sevens with their milk bottles and establishing William in his new wormery.

At prayer time she chose a hymn they all knew and then she quietly asked for the stories to be brought to her. Nine books were presented. The six- and seven-year-olds had all drawn colourful pictures of a house under the ground and written laboriously "William Worm lives here". They read this out and showed their pictures, then they sat down, smiling proudly. Paul and Peter had drawn identical pictures of a tree festooned with worms and written "William Worm found a worm tree and hung in it like a bat." Rita Lampton had carefully written up the story Abbie ·had told them with tiny illustrations beneath. Peter Edgehill and Stan Berrows had started a story which read like a lurid comic strip. Letty had put "William was a worm. I don't know what happened to him when he left home until tomorrow."

Hiding her smile with difficulty, Abbie thanked the children for their work and said simply, "Thank you, God, for minds and hands that can work like this and give us such joy. Please help us to go on working and enjoying our work. Please help us to look after your tiny creature, the worm."

Then she played another hymn and after a moment's silence sent the children into the playground.

It was a good start. Already the pattern for discussion and then individual work was set. After play the children did half an hour's work with numbers and then Abbie asked them to tidy up and settle around the piano for hymn practice while the dinner lady came in and laid the tables. She had no more trouble from Paul Enys and he shyly came to her with his number book while she was tying aprons on the small children. He was working from a much-thumbed and difficult text book and had completed a whole exercise correctly. Abbie was glad to be able to praise him.

"Oh, and Peter—" She called his brother over to her. "You obviously worked on your worm story together"— she didn't criticise this; separate ideas would come later with confidence gained—"and I liked the idea of William trying to be a bat. Think how you can go on with that. Will he try to fly, too? Or might a bird try to eat him?"

The boys had their heads together over their lunch and Abbie could hear Peter saying, "They might drop off the trees all at once and it would rain worms," and Rita Lampton scolding, "You are horrible—both of you—" while Letty Moran gave a subdued squeal and said she couldn't eat a thing.

During the afternoon she set the two older groups to paint and model, while she took the smaller ones for a reading lesson. There was a great deal of noise from the painting end, but she left them to it while she went with the others into the playground for a game with beanbags. At three she came back for story time only to find the clearing-up badly done and Rose Edgehill elbow-deep in filthy paint-pots in the wash basin.

"May I see the paintings, please? Yes, Marilyn, I can see most of them have been spoiled. What a pity. This one is worth saving—yours, Rita? Very nice. And this one, Matthew—" She ignored the tales being told and the shuffling Enys twins, and exhibited the good paintings, picking out their best points and noting various techniques. "If you will go and wash, you two, you may have the box of drawing pins from my desk and begin our Art Gallery—over here I think. Meanwhile, Rose and Peter can clear away the mess—no, thank you, Paul, two people can manage better alone. The rest of you sit in the book corner and we will choose a story."

Paul did not want to listen, he wanted to be busy. He shuffled and disturbed the others. Abbie finished the fairy story Alison Wyatt had chosen and picked up a book of poems in her own careful handwriting.

"We'll take it in turns to read a poem," she announced. "Paul, you're bored with listening. You have first turn."

He came smirking to her chair and took the book. They were simple poems about everyday things; she had written some of them herself, others had been written by former pupils. Paul read well but without expression. It was a poem about a cat.

"Try it again, Paul. Remember you're supposed to be the cat, so try to make your voice very soft, except when you're angry."

87

He glanced at the writing and then began again, more slowly and carefully, not trying to show off, but really listening to the words. At the end the children clapped. "I like that poem," he said. "May I copy it into my book, Mrs Eliot?"

"Of course." She was delighted and said without thinking, "Christopher wrote that. He made it up and I copied it down."

She felt his eyes glance up at her, then down to the poem again. He said nothing.

Mothers were already congregating at the playground gate. Abbie checked on the tidying and then sent the children for their outdoor clothes. They stacked their chairs on the tables and stood silently while she began the evening prayer, and then with one accord they joined in the last line—"Thank you, God, for *everything*!"

Abbie watched them file out of the classroom, already loving them, knowing that most of them would answer the question about the new teacher with a satisfyingly vague, "Mrs Eliot? Oh, she's all right."

So the first three weeks flew by with never a minute to spare. Mrs Thompson became her firm ally and Lady Margaret, who came two afternoons a week, suggested that she could manage practically any time if Mrs Eliot wanted to do anything special with a smaller group of children. Abbie got on very well with the aristocratic woman from the Hall; Lady Margaret was the ideal school helper, occupying herself with her allotted group and never interfering with the other activities. The children stood in great awe of her but knew it was a special honour to be in her embroidery class, and worked industriously at the table-cloths Abbie had tentatively suggested.

During her second weekend Mr and Mrs Dawes carried her off for another lunch at their bungalow, where Lady Margaret was also a guest. Mr Dawes was dishing up and pouring sherry at the same time. Lady Margaret watched suspiciously as he mopped a spill with a tissue. Already their mannerisms were familiar to Abbie and she smiled as she watched the ritual between husband and wife. "Arnold won't let me do a thing on a Sunday," said Mary Dawes, flying back and forth with cutlery and napkins and making certain her husband had everything to hand.

During lunch Mr Dawes suggested diffidently whether —after half-term of course, when things had settled into a routine—and only if Mrs Eliot was in full agreement —whether it might be possible for him to take the older group for Nuffield French?

Abbie was delighted. "It would give me time to get the middle group started off on a history project," she said. "I've ordered some books on Saxon and Roman times which they can use—"

"My dear, the expense—" Lady Margaret said, looking aghast—though whether at the sherry or Abbie's books it was hard to decide.

"From the Casterbridge library," Abbie explained. "I'll go in next Saturday and pick them up. We really should have the library van call at the school though."

"Frankly, we never got around to any . . . trimmings," Mr Dawes confessed. "For the last year our energies have gone almost entirely on simply keeping the school going."

Abbie smiled at him. "Well, things will certainly be different now. What between embroidery and French on the curriculum we begin to sound like a finishing school!"

Mrs Dawes came in and suggested she take a class on flower arranging, pointing to the same jar full of flop-headed dahlias in the grate. Everyone laughed.

When the short golden days of September were nearly at an end, the School Adviser—the old Inspector—arrived one morning and seated himself on one side of Abbie's desk while the morning story and discussion went on, then moved around from table to table watching progress. With the help of flash cards and pictures the little ones had quite an extensive vocabulary about William the Worm, who by now had a wife, sons, daughter and grandchildren, all making new tunnels in the wormery which had to be traced by little fingers and drawn in books. Paul and Peter had written a highly imaginative story in which their worm had travelled through time on bat wings, but as soon as the visitor paused by Paul he wrote quickly, "A big bird, probably a roc, pounced and William was gone. The End."

The Adviser was much younger than Abbie had thought possible. She judged him to be about twenty-six or seven with barely enough years to have gained the sort of experience he would need in his job. However, he gave Paul a sharp look at this and went on to the next table without any comment. Abbie, standing near by, said briskly, "Well, it had to end some time, Paul. Let's have a drawing of the roc, please." She took an early opportunity of discussing Paul's difficulties with her visitor, whom she suddenly suspected of being very much more aware of the situation than he seemed.

"He loathes painting," she confided. "There's always a mess when I let him near the easels, which is strange— or perhaps not too strange—when you consider his mother was an artist. Yet he can write the most marvellous poems and stories . . . it doesn't make sense."

"Give him some large modelling to do," suggested the Adviser. "A few big grocery boxes and some newspaper and plenty of paste. Ask him to make a giant roc and see what happens."

"That's an idea. Thank you . . . er . . ."

"Steve Bennett—sorry I haven't had a chance to introduce myself. It's a pleasure to be of help, Mrs Eliot. You're doing good work here. I'd like to see it go on. You realise you're on the danger list?"

"Yes, but I can't quite see why. The standard of work is as good as any I've seen in other schools, and though the equipment is old-fashioned, it's adequate."

"Numbers. If you lost another two or three, you'd have to close. So many parents already send their children to Castle Combe and they're badgering for a bus."

"Oh, dear."

"Normally I would suggest you see this boy's parents

91

and find out what's biting him. But if they go huffy and remove him and his twin, where would you be?"

Steve Bennett left at lunch-time. "If there's anything I can do, please telephone."

She grinned, "I contact County Hall on pain of death! Could you put us on the list for the library van, please? And what about the museum Service? I would like some Roman pottery—Saxon axes—things like that."

He was laughing. "Don't ring me, I'll ring you. There's a jolly good teacher's centre at Casterbridge, too. Perhaps you could get in on a Saturday and have a look round."

Abbie watched him drive away with some regret. He belonged to the outside world where teachers could command new books and equipment and the help of a psychologist for difficult pupils like Paul Enys. She watched him as he played in the September sun beneath the elm tree. The small girls had already learned to move their acorn-cup tea-sets away from his vicinity, but he wasn't interested in them today. It was conker time and Paul's quick eye and agile wrist made him a champion. He shouted raucously at his brother, "Got ya, Pete! My conker's beaten ten others now!" He did a war dance around the dinner lady and she drove him out into the open spaces of the playground.

Abbie sighed. Was she depriving Paul of expert help by coping alone with him, or was she in fact building up a background of security for him as she hoped? If she did ask the psychologist to call and observe him, he would almost certainly be removed, either officially or by an annoyed Daniel, and presumably that would be the end of Linstowel school.

She wandered slowly over to the school house to make herself some coffee before the afternoon session. She still hadn't bought a refrigerator and the milk smelt sour. She put it out on the table with margarine and flour. The top group were cooking this afternoon, and they could make a really big batch of scones. The first table-cloth would be finished today, and tomorrow they would lay a table at playtime with milk and lemon squash and the scones, and all have a mid-morning feast. If it went well it could be repeated at next week's Harvest Festival, when the Reverend Odgers was coming to take the service. But she really could do with a fridge. . . .

The telephone rang and her heart sank as she recognised Mr Lampton's voice. She had seen or heard nothing of him since their row on the day she moved in and apart from a brief note of thanks for her newly painted kitchen, she had tried not to think of either Lampton or Daniel.

"Thought I'd let you know Forrester can come first weekend in October and see to the stove," Lampton announced brusquely in her ear.

"Forrester? Oh, the blacksmith. Good. We might need some heat if this Michaelmas weather breaks."

There was a pause while Abbie debated whether to break the ice by mentioning the kitchen again. Then Lampton spoke.

"School Inspector came this morning then?"

93

Abbie's eyes widened. How on earth did he know so soon?

"Mr Bennett was most helpful," she said formally. "He is going to get us some museum exhibits—"

"You didn't complain about lack of funds?"

Abbie gripped the phone. "Of course not. There are various loan services for schools which it is up to us to use."

There was a Lampton grunt from the other end. "I'm not so sure. I've a feeling the quieter we keep down here, the better. No need to poke ourselves under their noses—"

"Oh, really, Mr Lampton, aren't you getting a little too edgy about the school?"

"Perhaps." He sounded almost conciliatory. "Actually I was going to mention something else . . ." He waited for encouragement, but getting none he went on hesitantly. "Miss Ritchie has arrived at the cottage, Mrs Eliot."

Abbie longed to be rude. Instead she said stonily, "I really do not see why that should interest me, Mr Lampton."

"Enys will be there with her. He always is. He—"

Abbie said furiously, "Mr Lampton, how dare you pester me with your narrow village gossip! I refuse to listen any more—kindly do not get in touch with me again unless it is strictly school business!"

"Wait a minute, Mrs Eliot. It is school business. I thought you should know because of the Enys boys . . . they'll be more difficult."

"You thought of that very quickly! You'll be pleased to know then that Paul and Peter have settled down. Any little troubles they had are all sorted out now. Goodbye, Mr Lampton."

Abbie put the telephone down with a decisive click.

Outside the children's voices floated to her through the open window of the study.

"Just you put that worm back again, Pete Enys—" It was Rita Lampton as usual, keeping an eye on things. "It's cruel to hang them up in the tree like that—"

Then Paul's voice, belligerent. "Go on, Pete—and another one! Mrs Eliot said it was a good idea, Rita Lampton, so there!"

Abbie went outside to sort them out. She wondered whether Lampton was right about Daniel and Margo Ritchie, and if so, how it would affect the two boys. She sighed again. Already Lampton's poisonous gossip was affecting her and she was seriously considering what he said. Yet would Daniel upset his sons—and presumably his mother—by openly living with another woman, however much she reminded him of his dead wife? Abbie clenched her hands, knowing that the thought hurt her personally.

FIVE

LADY MARGARET, the guest of honour at their "table-cloth celebration" the next day, declared she had never tasted such delicious scones before. Marilyn Thompson and Rose Edgehill smiled widely and little Janie announced in a loud voice that her sister had made them there cakes. Job Wyatt and Matthew Filbert, the male cooks of the top group, turned dull red and shuffled their feet.

Abbie said she would like to thank the cooks and the embroiderers. She hoped by next week the second cloth would be ready and then they would be used each day for school dinners.

"As you know, we are having our Harvest Thanksgiving next Wednesday afternoon. Your parents are invited and the school managers will be here." She smiled at Lady Margaret. "So let us give them all a feast like we've had today. . . . Now let us think about the scones we have just eaten. How did they come from God . . .?"

A discussion was soon under way. The Wyatt children said they could bring a sugar beet to show everyone how sugar started, and of course Rita could bring some wheat. It was decided that the middle group would paint an enormous cow. Their harvest gifts would be arranged around these things. Lady Margaret tentatively offered a cotton-head and some flax to show the beginnings of the table-cloths. As always, the children were full of enthusiasm.

On Friday evening Mrs Dawes telephoned to suggest that Abbie should accompany the two of them to Caster-bridge.

"The train service is so poor, my dear. Arnold and I drive in about once a month to shop and see a film, or even go to the theatre. Now don't say you're too busy—school teachers are always too busy. Mrs Enys was telling me in the shop the other day that you are planning to buy a refrigerator and Arnold is quite certain you will want to visit the teacher's centre, so why not combine the two?"

Abbie always used Saturdays for her chores; cleaning the cottage, shopping and laundering, washing her hair —all this took most of the day. Nevertheless she did need a fridge, and she really should visit the Centre . . .

"I'll come. Thank you very much, Mrs Dawes—"

"Mary."

"Thank you, Mary," Abbie laughed, grateful as she always was for the quiet support of the elderly couple.

She washed her hair then and there and telephoned Mrs Enys with a grocery list.

"You're going to Casterbridge then?" Mrs Enys sounded not at all her cheerful self. "I am glad. One gets . . . narrow . . . down here."

Had she heard the gossip about Daniel and Margo

Ritchie? Abbie said lightly, "You're almost immured, yet you manage to keep a good sense of proportion." There was no comment on this, so she went on, "Can I get you anything?"

"I did wonder whether I could ask you. Socks and pants for the boys? I don't even know the size. And it's Daniel's birthday next week. If I get him one of the big jerseys he likes from a chain store he could always change it . . ." There was something pathetically uncertain about this speech, coming from the definite Mrs Enys.

"Of course," said Abbie, wondering what Mr Lampton would say if he heard she was buying birthday presents for the Enys family. "I wish you could come, too. You sound tired and depressed."

"Daniel is away for the weekend and I am having the boys. As you know, they can be quite a handful." Mrs Enys gave a determined laugh so that Abbie would not take her too seriously.

"Oh." Abbie stared through the study window at the loaded apple tree. Her wet hair dripped on to the towel around her shoulders. For the life of her she could think of no comment to make. "Well . . . I'll get average sizes for the boys. That should do. And a large jersey?"

Mrs Enys laughed again and then said she would send Paul and Peter up with the groceries tomorrow evening.

Abbie put the telephone down slowly. It was an odd conversation to have with Mrs Enys. She towelled her hair vigorously, trying to think scornful thoughts about village gossip and its effect.

There was a tap on the kitchen door. It was Mrs Thompson.

"I've had a good go up at the school ready for the weekend, Mrs Eliot. And I was wondering . . . you haven't said nothing and I'm not one to push myself, but I always gave Miss Liddell a good turn-out on a Saturday . . ."

It seemed as if some of the drudgery was being taken out of the routine of Abbie's life. She smiled. "So that's why everything was so spick and span—clean paper in all the drawers—"

"Oh, yes, dear. I came in the day before and just worked around Miss Liddell and her young man. Couldn't have you coming into a messy cottage, could we?"

"Mrs Thompson, I'd be very pleased indeed. You can have the run of the place tomorrow because I'm off to Casterbridge for the day. How lovely it will be to come back and find everything done!"

"Well, I am glad about you going off for the day. I said to Mrs Wyatt, our Mrs Eliot's working too hard, I said—" Abbie felt warmed by the proprietary "our Mrs Eliot". She let Mrs Thompson have full rein while she made her a cup of tea. It seemed that Janie had come on a treat during her four weeks at school and was suddenly so independent! Abbie smiled. She was teaching Janie to tie her own shoe-laces—Janie had arrived in tie-up winter shoes on the first day when everyone else was wearing sandals—and she could manage buttons and write her own name now. It was a good start for a child who had been brought up to believe in her own invalidism.

Before Abbie came to Linstowel she wouldn't have thought she could ever enjoy an outing again as she enjoyed her Saturday in Casterbridge. The drive through the autumn-heavy countryside was a delight and as every mile made her feel almost physically lighter, Abbie realised the pressures she had been under since her arrival five weeks before. As always, the Dawes were the perfect hosts, Mary Dawes gay and carefree, Arnold Dawes quietly informative about landmarks and local history. The busy Saturday streets of the small country town were like a metropolis after Linstowel. It was a wonderful relief to walk along without being recognised and pointed out, to feel no sense of urgency—her chores were after all being done—to know that she couldn't possibly bump into Daniel or even the ludicrous Lampton.

She spent all morning choosing her refrigerator and buying Mrs Enys' commissions. Then she went straight to the dress department in the big chain store and bought herself a russet-brown light wool dress for the harvest festival. She met the Dawes for lunch and went off again to browse around the teachers' centre while they saw a film.

She was literally surrounded by books in the children's book department, when a voice spoke in her ear.

"It's Mrs Eliot, isn't it—from Linstowel?"

She looked round with surprise into the light brown intelligent eyes of Steve Bennett, the Schools Adviser.

"Mr Bennet—how nice. You see, I immediately took you up on your suggestion." She was genuinely pleased to see him. He was the kind of objective, uninvolved expert that Lampton would never believe existed in County officialdom.

"I rather hoped you'd let me fetch you over next weekend," he smiled back. "But now you're here, may I wean you from your books and show you the latest service we can offer—my particular enthusiasm actually—"

He led her through the audio-visual room to a small cubicle lined with boxes of tapes and equipped with a recorder and earphones.

"I've recorded every school programme that is put out," he told her enthusiastically. "And the Centre can lend a tape recorder too. Especially for schools without a radio or who would prefer to use programmes at other times."

Abbie was as thrilled as he was. She browsed through the catalogue he handed her and at last chose two programmes which would last the rest of the term if used weekly. One was about poetry—she admitted she had Paul Enys in mind when she chose that—the other was a musical series which combined mime and dance with musical appreciation.

"I'm hoping to produce video tapes of certain television programmes too," Steve Bennett went on. "There are one or two excellent Maths and Science series which would be of great help to your older groups."

"That would be marvellous—" They walked on through an art exhibition, talking animatedly. Probably because he was so much younger than she was, Abbie felt completely at ease with this man. Before she left, on a sudden impulse which she later regretted when she thought of Lampton's probable reaction, she invited Steve to their Harvest Festival.

"I'll try and make it," he promised. "I have to go to Castle Combe some time and I could fit it in then perhaps."

She would like Steve to see their harvest display and to have a chance to observe Paul and Peter again.

She met the Dawes in a restaurant for a cup of tea before the thirty-mile drive back. Besides the tapes and a recorder, she was struggling with a box of books and her morning's shopping. Mrs Dawes couldn't stop laughing and even Mr Dawes permitted himself a smile at the sight of so many bundles and boxes. Abbie's purchases and loans took up the whole of the boot of the car besides most of the back seat. Abbie sat tightly in one corner, infected by Mrs Dawes' laughter, and giggled happily. She felt like Rita and Letty with their new table-cloth.

The following week she managed to use one of the taped poetry programmes with great success. During Monday playtime Paul and Peter spent the whole of the twenty-minute break sorting through the books she had brought back and came up triumphantly with one of the broadcast poems. It was the Eleanor Farjeon one about cats.

"I could learn that," Paul boasted in his usual way. "I could learn that in about five minutes."

"Could you?" Abbie looked at him consideringly.

"Learn it tonight and let me hear it tomorrow and you can say it during our Harvest Thanksgiving."

He waited until Peter had dashed out to taunt Rita Lampton with this honour, then he said quietly, "I learned that poem that Christopher made up."

She stared at him. He must have slipped in during dinner hours and looked at the book she had carefully printed.

"Say it for me now, Paul. I should like to hear it."

His wary dark eyes took on a dreamy look as he visualised the poem. Then he began.

> "*I can pur—purr—purrrr*
> *And I can spit, like thisss, like thissss,*
> *I am soft as my soft fur,*
> *Then I'm hard and hiss, hiss, hissss!*"

He looked at her. "I'm like that. I wish I'd written that poem."

Abbie suddenly remembered his father, kind and cruel.

"Perhaps Christopher wrote it for you without even knowing," she said softly. "I'm glad you like it, Paul."

He hesitated, then he ran out to the others and she could hear his loud, boastful voice as he said the poem to an unwilling audience over and over again.

The following day neither he nor Peter were at school. She wondered whether to telephone and then didn't. Paul had taken the book of poetry home with him. Maybe he hadn't mastered it yet and was feigning illness until he did. In which case she was willing to go along a certain way for the sake of his pride.

Wednesday was a beautiful day, warm and golden, with the sun glinting off the distant sea like high summer. The children were busy during the morning, finishing their display with the fresh flowers and fruits they had brought from home and laying out their books for their parents to see during the afternoon. The top group laid the embroidered cloths on two tables and flitted across the playground from the school house bringing the scones they had made yesterday and a variety of Abbie's plates. They split scones and buttered them industriously. The middle group used the steps and pinned up their enormous cow collage and Abbie had the little ones around the piano practising their special piece.

After dinner they all assembled on the floor, leaving the chairs in serried ranks for their visitors. Abbie sent them in groups to wash and use the toilet, while she played action rhymes with the others and read them a story.

There was still no sign of the Enys boys and she was relieved in a way. She always had to keep an eye on Paul and he could generally be relied upon to disturb the little ones. On the other hand it would be a disappointment to him to miss saying the poem he had learned—or would it? It occurred to her that nerves about the poem could be a reason for his absence.

However, as the parents and managers began to arrive, she had to push such thoughts to the back of her mind. She let the children join their parents for a few minutes to show them around the decorated school room and point out their own personal pile of work, then she began to play the first verse of their harvest hymn very softly as a signal to take their places. It was a joy to see Janie push Mrs Thompson into a seat with a loud remonstrance to "please be very quiet, our Mum, else you're going to miss the nice bits".

As she turned to the children and reminded them of the first line, she was surprised to see Mrs Enys slip in from the playground and sit quietly with the parents in the back row. Behind her, Steve Bennett appeared and smiled warmly across the heads at her.

The service went well. Mr Odgers used simple prayers that the children could understand and took the trouble to mention each item of work displayed around the room. Afterwards the top group stood up without prompting and carried around plates and serviettes and their trays of scones. There were raised eyebrows among the mothers, nods and smiles of approbation, then near-tears of sentiment as the little ones piped up with their special offering. Alison Wyatt began.

"Thank you for our nice scones." Then came Miles Filbert, "Here is the sugar beet that made the sugar." Janie warbled, "And the wheat that made the flour," Stephen said gruffly. "And that's a picture of the cow who gives us the milk and butter." They waited for Abbie's signal, then they all burst out, "Thank you for all the food we eat every day."

It was some time before Abbie could find her way to Mrs Enys and then it was only to find that she knew nothing of the boys' absence.

"Paul was thrilled to bits on Monday about reading the poem," said his grandmother, looking anxious. "I can't imagine anything simple like a cold making him miss that."

"Probably his father would put his foot down if the boys are off colour," Abbie suggested.

Mr Odgers was waiting to make his farewells and then Steve Bennett wanted to congratulate Lady Margaret on her embroiderers, so she had to leave Mrs Enys. When she looked around the room later, she had gone.

Mr Lampton was among the last to leave. Eyeing Steve Bennett with great suspicion, he said to Abbie, "The children have certainly been busy, Mrs Eliot. Pity they haven't done a bit more on the three R's though."

Before Abbie could recover from that, he added in a low voice, "I see the Enys boys aren't here. What did I tell you? I knew there'd be trouble." He lifted his shooting hat. "Good day to you, Mrs Eliot. Forrester will be here on Saturday, so please be around to let him into the school."

Abbie stared after him almost venomously. Was there ever such a man for turning her feelings of pride and gratification to impotent fury? She turned with relief to Steve to thank him for coming and to tell him about the success of her first taped programme.

"I enjoyed every minute, Abbie—" When had he started calling her that? She hadn't noticed, yet it seemed quite natural. "Couldn't we please go on talking like this over a meal one day. This Saturday—I could pick you up—"

"Oh, I'd enjoy that. I do miss other teachers so much. But I can't manage it this weekend . . . that is unless the blacksmith comes early . . ."

He was laughing. "One-teacher schools certainly need dedicated teachers," he said. "Listen, if you can fix it with your blacksmith, telephone me. All right? I'm in the book."

She turned to make other farewells. How marvellous to have a friend like Steve Bennett, full of all the latest ideas, yet practical and understanding.

Lady Margaret was saying deeply, "Congratulations, Mrs Eliot. A most successful afternoon."

"Please take at least half the credit, Lady Margaret. We both know I couldn't manage without you now."

The lined face flushed with pleasure, but all she said was, "Egg cosies next, I think. For Christmas presents."

"Marvellous," smiled Abbie.

At last it was over and she was sitting with her feet up in her own little sitting-room, drinking tea and gloating at the new fridge humming away in the kitchen. It must have arrived some time during the afternoon and Mrs Thompson had superintended its installation. In fact she was in a mood to gloat about several things, when, as if to jolt her back to earth, the telephone rang. She groaned as she went into the study in her stockinged feet. If only it could be Mrs Dawes with an invitation to Sunday lunch. But somehow she knew it wasn't.

Mrs Enys' voice trembled a little as she greeted her. "Abbie? Are you alone, my dear? I went straight down to the inn to enquire about the boys and Tammy had no idea they had been away from school. They leave every morning at eight thirty and arrive home just after four."

Abbie said slowly, "Oh dear. Have you talked to them?"

"They were on the beach, fishing. I didn't have the heart."

"What did . . . what did their father say?"

There was a momentary pause. "He's not at home. He's away this week."

"I see." Abbie thought quickly. "We must hear what the boys have to say. We must be fair. If Tammy tells them off or . . ." She did not want to mention Daniel's uncertain moods. "They may well feel unbearably wronged—"

Mrs Enys sounded near tears. "Abbie, I hate to ask this, but the boys—they're so stubborn with me and I really feel I cannot cope. I wondered whether you could possibly tackle them."

Abbie said, "You know I want to help. I'm very fond of the boys and I feel they are gaining confidence, but I am very unwilling to interfere."

Mrs Enys said simply, "Please, Abbie. You're the only one. You're the right one. They'll listen to you."

"All right . . ." What else could she say? She cut short Mrs Enys' thanks. "Don't thank me until you see how it turns out. I'll phone or call in on my way back."

"I'll be waiting."

Abbie swallowed the rest of her tea and slid a

cardigan over her new brown dress. She kept telling herself that as Daniel wasn't at home she had nothing to worry about in talking to the boys. Nevertheless she set off for the Lobster Pot with a sinking feeling in the pit of her stomach.

Mrs Enys must have telephoned Tammy and the familiar bent figure of the old sea-cook was waiting in the doorway of the inn for her. As she had avoided coming along the slipway since her first day in Linstowel, she had not met up with Tammy at all and was surprised at the unadulterated pleasure she felt in seeing him again.

"Mrs Eliot!" His face was the colour of tobacco and split by a huge grin. "You haven't changed a bit since that holiday. I was that glad to hear you'd got the job up at the school. You helped him before and you can help him again."

Abbie was taken aback by his directness.

"Hang on, Tammy. You must know I can't do anything for Mr Enys. It's the boys that are my concern."

"They're waiting for you, my dear. But flowers will drop off a plant however carefully tended, if the roots dry up."

"Oh, Tammy. I'd forgotten your sayings! It really is good to see you again. Christopher loved you—" It was the second time she had mentioned Christopher casually like that recently. First to Paul and now to Tammy.

"I'm that sorry about them both, my dear. Your lovely boys. But you've got nothing to reproach yourself about. Your wound is clean and it'll heal."

109

Abbie frowned. "Tammy, what—"

"Come along in now. They're that worried about seeing you. Be easy on them."

He ushered her into a little room that looked out on to the harbour. Paul and Peter sat in a window seat, neatly brushed and clean like two small puppies. Their apprehension filled the tiny room. Abbie sat down facing them and waited.

Paul burst out defiantly, "We don't have to come to school if we don't want to—it's a waste of time!"

There was another silence.

"D'you agree with that, Peter?" asked Abbie.

"Yes—" Peter said gruffly.

"Tell me what you've been doing the last two days."

"Fishing—"

"C'llecting shells for the nature ta—just c'llecting shells."

"Exploring along the cliffs."

Abbie held up her hand and itemised their answers.

"Finding out what's in the sea. Finding out what's on the shore. Finding out what's along the cliffs." She looked up. "You've been finding out things. What do you think school is for? Now honestly—no silly answers. Peter, you first. What do we do at school?"

"We find things out," he said unwillingly.

Paul said triumphantly, "We can do that by ourselves. We don't need to come to school."

"Oh, yes you do. You'd miss such a lot of finding out on your own. You'd miss what other people found out too. Can you remember when you first discovered two and two made four?"

"I always knew that," Paul said scornfully.

"No you didn't. Neither did Matthew Filbert. But if you'd been at school this morning when your group were pinning up their cow picture, you would have heard him finding it out. He said—'Look, everyone, the cow's got two back legs and two front legs, that's four altogether'."

"So what?" said Paul.

Peter grinned. "That was funny . . ." He began to repeat Matthew's words. "That's good that is. I suppose there is a time for finding out something like that."

"Shut up, Pete—"

"You can't keep shutting people up, Paul. Not for long. Didn't you want to find out what everyone thought of the cat poem you were going to read?"

"Didn't anyone else do it? Rita knew it."

"She didn't tell me. It was your special poem. No one else would have read it."

There was another silence and then Abbie began to tell them about the afternoon. She finished up, "The little ones weren't a bit shy. You would have been proud of them."

Tammy knocked and came in with three cups of tea and a plate of biscuits.

Paul said, "Would you like to see our shells?"

Tammy winked broadly.

Abbie drank her tea and examined the shell collection with interest, then got up to go.

"There is one thing, boys. We don't want to worry your father about this. So we say nothing. All right?"

She expected relief and was surprised when the boys flashed each other a look of disappointment. She went home with the feeling that Tammy was right and she had not in fact got to the root of the trouble. Mrs Enys' gratitude was almost embarrassing in the circumstances.

The next day the boys were unusually quiet, almost sullen. It didn't help that the others couldn't stop talking about yesterday's "feast". In the effort to make them special, Abbie put them first in the line to go home and said in a low voice, "You kept our little secret, boys?"

They exchanged glances. "Dad's still at Aunty Margo's, so it wasn't too difficult," Paul said with adult sarcasm.

Abbie felt herself flushing as she sent the children off. So it was true. How could Daniel allow himself to be gossiped about . . . and that his own children should know.

The next day, Friday, when the boys were again absent, Abbie knew their anger was not directed against school or herself, but against their father. It had been so obvious, yet she hadn't seen it. After the death of their mother, the boys had needed Daniel more than ever, yet he had been unable to share his grief with them, because—according to Tammy—he was poisoned by remorse. She remembered Arnold Dawes' words that last Sunday morning in August when they had sat together on the cliff edge; hadn't he said something about Ghislaine Enys dying in peculiar circumstances? And hadn't Lampton hinted that Ghislaine had been unhappy, shutting herself away for long periods in the cliff cottage? Abbie had considered it right to ignore such allusions to the past, but now she wasn't so sure. If she knew a little more perhaps she could help the boys.

She left Mrs Thompson to clear up the school for the weekend and wandered over to the cottage, intending to repeat last Friday's programme of washing her hair and telephoning a grocery order to Mrs Enys in case she was able to see Steve Bennett tomorrow. However, she went on thinking about the problem of the boys, wondering how far she could go in her capacity as their teacher without trespassing on Daniel's right to a private life—however unsuitable she considered that life to be.

She tried to imagine what she would do if the problem arose with the Wyatts, and knew she would plunge in up to her neck to help the children if they were caught up in adult difficulties. Yet even if she knew how to get hold of Daniel, would she have the nerve to talk to him about his boys after what he had said to her? He would simply accuse her again of trying to keep the twins at school for the sake of her own job.

She made up her mind suddenly and picked up her shopping list and a basket. She would collect her own groceries right now and try to find an opening to talk to Mrs Enys.

It was only a few minutes before five when she reached the general store and she rushed inside before

Mrs Enys could drop the latch on her last customer. After the golden sunlight, the shop seemed very dark and it took Abbie a few seconds to realise that there were two other customers in the shop. One was Daniel and the other must be Margo Ritchie.

Abbie had carefully avoided all contact with Daniel since their last turbulent meeting, and she supposed that he had done his best to avoid her too. Now the shock of his presence was startling. Again there was the peculiar sense of recognition . . . if only they could have been friends. . . . Now, after Daniel's brutal embrace, this curious feeling of being linked was given a physical awareness too. Abbie was conscious of the space between them, conscious that it would be dangerous to move closer to him.

And somehow, at the root of their strange antagonism, there was this woman. Margo Ritchie, friend of Ghislaine Enys, who might well be part of the "peculiar circumstances" which surrounded Ghislaine's death.

She was a small woman, probably in her late twenties, but with the haggard good looks of the over-sensitive which made her look very much older in many ways. Her hair, dark and sticky with sea salt, lay damply on her navy-blue smock and her jeans and rope-soled sandals were soaking.

She was talking to Mrs Enys in a low, lilting voice, but without any laughter in it.

"Your son told me I needed a cold shower. So I just took off my smock and went in. Now he complains because some stodgy old farmers were watching . . ."

Abbie wondered if one of the stodgy old farmers could be Lampton. She also wondered why Margo Ritchie might have needed a cold shower. And why she told this amusing little anecdote in such a curiously flat, humourless way.

Daniel had been as aware of Abbie as she had been of him and he took Margo's arm before she finished speaking.

"We must go. Come on." He used no endearment.

Margo shrugged free. "I have to take the coffee with me. Black coffee is what I need. What we both need—" She shot a look at Daniel and he seized her arm again.

"Come on, I said—"

Mrs Enys, whose silence through all this told only too clearly of her unhappiness—Mrs Enys was never silent—tried to rescue the situation.

"Abbie!" she said in an unnaturally high voice. "I didn't see you—" She lifted the counter flap. "Come on through, I'm nearly finished." She hesitated a moment and then added, "I don't think you know Miss Ritchie. This is Mrs Eliot, Margo."

The dark eyes met Abbie's. They were not just unhappy eyes, Abbie realised with a sense of shock, they were haunted.

"You stayed in the cottage for a couple of nights, didn't you? You were welcome. Lonely dump, isn't it?" Still no smile to lighten the words.

"Yes, it is rather," Abbie agreed. "But it was a very comfortable port in a storm."

At last there was a laugh. Short and bitter.

115

"Yes. I'll grant you that." She glanced back at Daniel standing uncomfortably behind her. "A port in a storm, eh, Danny boy?"

"Come on, Margo," he repeated a little more gently. "Mrs Eliot has shopping to do." He bundled a cardboard box under his arm as Margo shrugged and lifted a small hand in a mock salute to Abbie and then sauntered squelchily out of the shop. Daniel hesitated.

"Cheerio, Mother. You'll have the boys for the week-end then."

"Yes—" Mrs Enys turned suddenly and went through to her parlour.

"Abbie," Daniel looked past her to where Margo lingered in the sun-filled street. "My mother told me what you did for Paul and Peter. You know how grateful I am. We started off on the wrong foot and I cannot burden—anyone—with my difficulties. But—" his dark eyes flicked over her face and away. "I've no right to ask you—keep an eye on the boys for me. Please." Margo's low voice called irritably, and he added hurriedly, "And my mother. She's upset."

She stared at him. The dark hair and beard made him look like one of the smugglers he had described to Chris and the twins that halcyon summer a lifetime ago, and she could believe he was the kind of man even in this day and age who would take the law into his own hands. And she was the village school teacher, a symbol of civilisation and law and order! And then she remembered the scratch meal he had made her that day at the cottage, and the admonition to air the sheets. He had cared for her then, even though he thought she was a stupid fool who had run out on her family in a moment of petty anger. And afterwards, after he had whipped her with his scorn and tried to show her what the loss of Ghislaine had done to him, even then he had telephoned her at the school house and said, "Are you all right?"

She said in a stifled voice, "Of course I'll keep an eye on them. And your mother." Something made her add, "But please take care."

His hand was warm on hers. The small gesture of gratitude made her gasp and he smiled wryly, understanding. Then he was gone.

She stood still for a moment, her whole being reeling with this tacit admission of physical attraction. She had come to talk over a problem with Mrs Enys; diffidently, tentatively, she had approached the situation, holding herself tightly in control as usual, trying to deal with one thing at a time. Now she was different. Impossible to say how. But in spite of everything—Margo Ritchie, the obvious nerve-twanging tension, Mrs Enys' sudden breakdown, the twins' truancy and the difficulties at school—she was aware that she was alive again. After nearly two years of existing, she was alive. It hurt. But it was a kind of triumph.

She shook herself mentally and went through the opened counter and into the little back room.

Mrs Enys stood with her hand on the mantelpiece and her head bowed. She looked round at Abbie's entrance and tried to smile.

117

"I'm sorry, my dear. You seem to be pitchforked into our troubles through no fault of your own—"

"I want to help, Mrs Enys. I came here to talk to you about the boys—"

"The boys seem the least of Daniel's worries at the moment, Abbie. Is he bewitched by Margo? I simply cannot understand." She broke down finally and Abbie held her in her arms, feeling a surge of strength she hadn't known she possessed. Now was not the time to tell their grandmother that the boys had again skipped school; she could deal with that alone somehow. She encouraged the old lady to sit down while she made tea, and then she lit a fire in the empty grate against the early September evening and went through to lock up the shop. After being determined to keep out of Daniel's affairs, she was now prepared to become totally involved in them.

She settled down opposite Mrs Enys and said bluntly, "I want to know everything there is to know about Ghislaine's death, please, Mrs Enys. How is Margo involved? Is Daniel in love with her—and how much do the boys know of all this? Please don't hold anything back. I've got to know if I'm to help at all."

Mrs Enys looked surprised for a moment as she sipped her tea, then she sighed deeply and put the cup and saucer down.

"Abbie, you've heard the same kind of gossip I've heard. I know nothing else. I wish Daniel would talk to me—heaven knows I've asked him often enough. Perhaps he wants to spare me."

"Exactly how did Ghislaine die?"

"She went over the cliff opposite the cottage. Her body was found in that small pebbly cove. The Coroner's verdict was Death by Misadventure."

Abbie's heart thumped. It must be the cove she had climbed into that first Sunday. No wonder Arnold Dawes had been rather shattered when he came upon her.

She said brutally, "Was it suicide?"

"My dear, I don't know. There was no note, nothing." Mrs Enys sighed and picked up her cup and saucer. "Abbie, I'll admit to you I never got on with Ghislaine. When the marriage started to crack up I was sorry for Daniel, but I really thought it might be for the best in the end. She couldn't have been faithful to anyone for long . . ." She sipped her tea slowly as she stared into the fire and into the past. "I went back to the North when my husband died. It was my old home and I thought I'd be happier there. The truth was, I couldn't bear to watch Ghislaine's behaviour. Daniel bought that cottage from Charlie Lampton and fitted it up as a studio for her, and you can imagine . . . oh, Abbie, it was a rotten situation. Margo was the only one who could do anything with her at times. She used to come down and stay in the cottage with her—she's a serious painter—and during those times, Ghislaine was calm and loving towards the boys. And I always thought that Daniel was . . . just grateful to Margo."

"Was Margo at the cottage when Ghislaine died?" Abbie asked suddenly.

"No. She didn't turn up for months. Daniel wasn't too bad at first. There was gossip, of course—"

"Everyone thought Ghislaine had committed suicide?"

"Not really. I came to stay—I must have just missed meeting you and your family—and Daniel himself said he didn't think Ghislaine was the type to jump over cliffs. . . . No, the gossip was worse than that. There had been terrible rows between them—between Daniel and Ghislaine. He has a temper—"

"I know. I can imagine. Go on."

"People had heard the rows. He threatened her—he wouldn't hurt a fly when it came to it, Abbie—but he was heard to say he'd kill her if she was unfaithful to him again. The next day her body was found in the cove." The tea-cup clattered in its saucer. "You must have heard this, Abbie—surely you haven't been spared."

"Someone has tried to tell me," Abbie said grimly. "I refused to listen."

"Well, of course, I took no notice. Not then. Daniel was convinced it was an accident himself. If he'd thought it was suicide he'd have felt hideously responsible, but he honestly did not believe Ghislaine was capable. He said gossip would die a natural death. They were getting on fine. Better than . . . before. So I went home. Then I had a letter from Mary Dawes. Apparently Margo turned up. She was ill. At first Daniel and Tammy looked after her at the inn. Then for some reason he took her up to the cottage. After a week she disappeared again and Daniel came home.

120

But he was different. Morose and moody. He pulled himself together for a time. Then she arrived again and exactly the same thing happened." Mrs Enys' voice trembled. "I came down and Daniel told me to go back home, he was taking no more guests. He said that—to his own mother. So last winter I bought this business, and I've tried . . . I've tried . . ." Tears came again and Abbie crouched by the chair, stroking the white hair, deep in thought herself. So much was explained. So much was still completely inexplicable.

At last Mrs Enys lifted her head.

"Abbie, I couldn't say this to anyone else. But there is an explanation that fits. If Daniel did . . . kill Ghislaine that night and somehow Margo knows, they may well be bound together by something more terrible, more compelling than attraction or even love." The grey eyes met Abbie's startled blue ones. "I'm so frightened, my dear. Every time I see them together I become more convinced—I dream about it. Abbie, I'm beginning to believe my own son is capable of murder."

SIX

ABBIE spent a long evening trying to think constructively about what Mrs Enys had told her, and only in so far as it might affect Paul and Peter. This was difficult; she found she had small control over her racing mind. At one stage she actually lifted the phone to ring Tammy and ask him if he could arrange a meeting between herself and Daniel so that she could thrash the matter out once and for all. She stopped herself in time, uncertain of her true motives. Deeper than her concern for the welfare of the boys was an urgent desire to see Daniel for her own sake. Not only to find the truth, but to be in the live warmth of his presence; to feel her isolation a thing of the past and to assure him that she would help. Yet . . . supposing he had killed his wife. What then? Could she honestly feel anything but horror for him?

At last she decided to seek some outside advice. She thought of Steve Bennett with relief. It was his job to advise her anyway and she knew that already his friendship would extend beyond mere duty. What was more, she respected his know-how and his sensitivity. She could trust him with this delicate situation.

She flipped open the directory and found his number.

"Steve?" It was the first time she had used his Christian name, but she felt unable to ask for Mr Bennett. "It's me. Abigail Eliot from Linstowel school. I know it's late—"

"Abbie—of course it's not. But if you're ringing to tell me the blacksmith is coming between us, it's much too late. I've already booked our luncheon table at the Golden Hind."

"Oh, Steve. How marvellous—" She had actually forgotten about the blacksmith and the proposed lunch with Steve. Daniel's problem had driven everything else from her mind. She thought quickly. The blacksmith must take care of himself and she would save her problems to tell Steve over their meal. "I was telephoning to confirm that I could come. I'll catch the eleven o'clock from here—it's due in before mid-day. Is that all right?"

"Of course—I'll meet you. Till then."

"Good night, Steve. And thank you."

"Good night, Abbie. God bless."

It was a tender farewell. She reflected for an instant that he was as fond of her as she was of him. Maybe she would have felt this way towards a younger brother if she had ever had one. Then her mind went back like tired clockwork to the things Mrs Enys had told her. She thought of the beautiful Ghislaine, who had left an impression of tragedy behind her so that even Lampton had said that she'd had to get away by herself . . . it didn't sound like a faithless wife. More like an unhappy and neglected one. Perhaps there had been friendships with other men . . . then the short-tempered husband shouting that he would kill her. . . . Abbie could understand so well how the talk had started. And she could almost believe it, even as Mrs Enys was beginning to believe it, if she didn't know Daniel.

She sighed sharply. She had relied on her instinct about Daniel before and had been hurt.

The next day there was a feeling of winter in the air. Abbie hadn't slept well and she went outside at half past seven to clear her head. The last of the apples were on her tiny lawn and the sprout plants Stan Berrows and Peter Edgehill had planted much too late looked limp and unhappy in the first frost of the year. She picked up the apples, thinking that perhaps Lady Margaret could take a small group into the fields to pick the last of the blackberries and they could make bramble jelly in the next cooking class. It was strange how another half of her mind could plan ahead like this. She was seeing the top group after school on Monday to hold their first recorder session. . . .

By eight o'clock she had washed and set her hair on a sudden impulse. She always pinned it severely behind her ears as befitted a school teacher, but her day in Casterbridge last weekend had made her feel distinctly unfashionable. She laid her new brown dress on the bed and a bright yellow silk scarf to go with it. Later on, if the sun came out she wouldn't need a coat. Meanwhile she sat in front of the electric fire while her hair dried, and read Letty Moran's latest work which began, "I never know what to rite about unless I sit by

Rita and Ime sitting by Stephen Tanner today to look after him. He's a little boy with funy hair but I like him bekase he is going to marry me if Peter Edgehill wont." Abbie chuckled as she unpinned her hair and brushed it in to a pale cloud around her face. Letty rarely wrote anything without using the words "marriage" and "engagement". Her one ambition at the moment was to be a bridesmaid and to this end she watched her older brother and sister closely.

There was a knock at the front door and Abbie hurried to answer it, hoping it would be Mr Forrester the blacksmith. It was Lampton. Abbie tried to feel more tolerant towards him, perhaps his attitude was more understandable. She led him into the sitting-room and offered him coffee.

His pale blue eyes were more protuberant than usual as he took in the brown dress and gay yellow scarf.

"You look different, Mrs Eliot—" Could it possibly be a compliment for Lampton? "Is it your hair? You haven't combed it yet."

"I have in fact brushed it into a new style," Abbie said gently, practically forcing him into her armchair. "The coffee is perking so please sit down, Mr Lampton." She was tempted to tell him to take off his hat, but perhaps that sounded too much like a school teacher. "Was it about the blacksmith? We shall have to light the stove if this frosty weather is here to stay."

"Yes. Yes, we shall that." He seemed to have forgotten what he was going to say. Of his own accord he took off his checked cap and put it awkwardly on his lap. Abbie poured him some coffee and smiled at him encouragingly.

"He should be here about eleven. The blacksmith that is."

Before Abbie could tell him she was catching the morning train he blurted out, "How have the Enys boys been?"

"Oh—" she said cautiously. "On the whole they're improving, I think. Paul is very interested in poetry and Peter's favourite subject is natural science—"

"They skipped school again on Friday."

"Yesterday? Yes, they were absent. I noticed they were both starting colds."

"Rubbish. You know as well as I do they were playing truant."

"We neither of us know that, Mr Lampton."

"Well, I certainly do. I saw them fishing down in the cove—"

Abbie's heart seemed to jump into her throat. "The cove by the cottage?"

"Yes. I often walk along that way. They'd clambered down just where—" he broke off and took a mouthful of coffee.

"Just where their mother fell off the cliff," Abbie finished slowly.

Lampton put his cup down and went back to fiddling with his hat. "I walked up to the cottage to tell Enys. It's not right two little kids like that, down there on their own. But he wasn't there, and when I shouted to them both boys went conveniently deaf. They're little devils when they want to be."

"They are," Abbie felt bound to agree.

"I came on into the village to let Tammy know where they were. And there was that—hussy—going into the sea half-naked and Enys just watching her. I don't care if you order me out again, Mrs Eliot, but that man isn't fit to have children in his care."

In spite of her immediate anger, Abbie had to admit it was a valid point of view and one she might have shared in different circumstances.

She said slowly, "He said himself—some time ago—that he was thinking of sending them to boarding school."

Lampton looked at her sharply. "That would be the end of the school then. I suppose you agree with him?"

"No, I don't think I do. Their behaviour is directed at him, not at school. They're really much better behaved now in school. I think they want to shock their father into noticing them. If he sent them away it would merely confirm their fear that he wanted to forget them."

"But surely he does—"

"Not really. He thinks they're well looked after—his mother is here and Tammy lives in after all. His absences are only occasional—"

"When he's occupied with—that woman."

"Miss Ritchie is an old friend. She knew his wife—"

"D'you think I don't know that? Poor Ghislaine—

how she must have suffered." Abbie stared at him. His clown's face was tragically sad.

She said gently, "We don't know what kind of torture Mr Enys is suffering. Our concern is how it is affecting his children. Do *you* think they should go to boarding school?"

"For their good, yes. But I don't want to lose our school. It means a lot to me to keep this village alive and the school is our only—institution. Even the church is a part-time affair now."

"Mr Lampton, I think for once we really are of the same mind. We do not know what to do for the best—"

He interrupted fiercely. "*I* know what to do, Mrs Eliot. Keep this whole sordid business to ourselves. That's one of the reasons I'm here. I was worried to see that Inspector at the service on Wednesday afternoon. He's snooping, Mrs Eliot—he's either heard something or he noticed the boys' behaviour, and if it goes any further we both know what will happen."

"Mr Bennett came to school on Wednesday at my invitation. And how can you talk like this, Mr Lampton, if you honestly believe the boys' best interest would be served by a boarding school?"

"Because they're just two children as against fifteen others, Mrs Eliot. Get your priorities straight."

Abbie stared at him in silence. Perhaps he was right. She wondered whether the other managers would agree with him. The Reverend Odgers would not, but she was unsure about Lady Margaret and Mr Dawes. How badly she needed Steve's objectivity!

She picked up Lampton's empty coffee cup. "You must excuse me, Mr Lampton. I am catching the eleven o'clock train into Casterbridge."

"What about the blacksmith?" Lampton protested.

Abbie took a key from the top of the sideboard. "Here is the school key. Perhaps you can hand it over and tell him to push it through the letter box when he has finished. If not, Mrs Thompson will arrive in a moment to clean the cottage and she will let him in."

Lampton stood up disgruntled, and put on his cap. "I thought you'd had a day out last weekend. Dawes said you went Christmas shopping."

A devil appeared in Abbie's blue eyes. "I had to buy a birthday present for Daniel Enys. But I did no Christmas shopping. Today I am meeting Mr Bennett for lunch. I want to discuss with him the problem of the Enys twins." She swept ahead of him and opened the front door. "Are you coming or staying, Mr Lampton?" she finished sweetly.

He closed his mouth. "I'll go and wait over in the school," he said in a surly voice. "You know what I think about discussing our business with outsiders. But you'll take no notice of me, of course." He paused as he went past her. "I'm thinking of you as well as the school, Mrs Eliot. You're doing a fine job. It'll be a crying shame if you can't go on with it."

Abbie watched him plod up the playground and shook her head wryly. He was the most contrary man she had ever met. Besides Daniel of course.

129

Lunch at the Golden Hind in Casterbridge was a pleasant, leisurely affair. Steve had left what he called his "office suit" at home and was wearing a hairy tweed jacket that made him look even younger. Abbie teased him and said he looked like a schoolboy in his father's clothes and he coloured slightly and protested, "I am twenty-nine you know, Abbie, just how old are you?"

"Such a question! I'm thirty-three."

"Just four years older than I am. Does it make you feel safe to pretend you're a different generation?"

She felt momentarily confused. "I *am* a different generation really, Steve. My tenth wedding anniversary was last month and my son would be eight years old now." She smiled at him a little mistily. "That's the first time I've said anything like that without breaking up."

He reached across the table and touched the back of her hand lightly. "Well done," he said. She felt like a queen.

As if to give her a chance to recover, he began to tell her about his life.

"You must think it odd that I've reached the ripe age of twenty-nine without marrying—" His clear brown eyes grinned at her. "Frankly, Abbie, I've been too busy. After I got my degree I spent a year getting an Education Diploma, then I taught for two years—history at a school in the Midlands, and I found I was doing a lot of unofficial counselling for the teenagers there. So I went on a course and became an Educa-

tional Psychologist, and I'd been doing that for a couple
of years when I had this offer. I think I'll stay here for
a while and try to get some roots put down."

"Mark called it a grass roots place."

"I know what he meant. There's something basic,
elemental about the coastline. A constant reminder of
the sheer puniness of our efforts at civilisation and
sophistication."

"Yes." Abbie found she was again thinking of
Daniel; the untamed wild part of his nature. "That
reminds me, Steve, I would like to talk over a school
matter. Your experience as a psychologist would be
invaluable if you could bear to listen."

"Of course, what am I here for? Those twins is it?
The fierce one . . . Paul."

"You remember them. Were they so bad then?"

"Not really. I've seen much worse. But the seeds were
there. The beginnings of total rebellion against our
system. Rather like the elemental quality we discussed
in the coastline. It's there in every one of us and our
ability to cope with life depends to a large extent on our
ability to control that side of our nature."

What chance did Paul have with a father like Daniel
and a wayward mother like Ghislaine?

Steve went on, "This is where school is so important.
It must link with home, but it must offer another view
of life as well. If you like, it can counteract the inevitable effects of heredity!" He laughed. "Sounds pom-
pous, doesn't it?"

"No, not really. School is just far enough away that

131

you can turn around and see yourself and your family objectively."

"Exactly. But if you're like Paul and Peter you mustn't go too far. You lose sight of them then, and they either become romanticised in memory, or even hated."

Abbie sighed. "Well, that's answered the immediate problem straightaway. You see, the home is broken and disturbed at the moment. The father has been considering boarding school and recently there have been cases of truancy."

Steve said acutely, "School is enabling them to see they're getting unfair treatment and they're protesting in the only way they can. If they were at home they might not see what was wrong, but they would be extremely unhappy. Probably more so than now."

"That might well be. I don't know. My problem was whether I was trying to cope with them at the village school for their sake or for my own. If they both left it would probably be the end of Linstowel Primary."

"Keep them for the time being. Tell the father it's their best hope."

"Sorry, Steve, that's out. I can't talk to the father."

"Oh. A great pity. Then you must talk to the boys. Try to show them that what they are doing is against their own interests. Use modern jargon. Tell them to play it cool for a while."

Abbie grinned. "Paul would like that." She pulled on her yellow scarf. "Thank you, Steve. It helps enormously to discuss things with you because you're so objective."

"It's not always easy." He watched her as she tied the scarf. "Your hair is the colour of that silk, Abbie. I could easily stop being objective—"

"Steve, stop it!" Abbie laughed but coloured slightly.

"—And take you back to Linstowel," he went on deliberately. "Meet your two troublemakers and talk to them myself. With my special voice of authority—"

Abbie stopped fiddling with her scarf. "Oh, Steve. Would you?"

"And then you would feel bound to give me a genteel tea—perhaps we could light a fire—and then we could sit and talk about something else besides schools—"

"Oh, Steve, if you would—they'd listen to you; it would make it seem so serious with the School Inspector arriving—"

"Adviser, please, Abbie."

"Well, everyone calls you the Inspector at Linstowel and they're all frightened to death of you."

"Thanks."

Somehow they were both laughing and he was shepherding her out of the hotel with an arm around her shoulders. She decided to telephone Tammy so that he could round up the boys and send them to the school house about four. Daniel was still "away" of course. She sighed. For an hour she had imagined she had forgotten him in concern for his sons.

They arrived back at the house at half past three. Abbie was touched and delighted to find Mrs Thompson had lit the first fire of the autumn and drawn up the low table which she had laid for Abbie's tea.

"One thing I did not learn at College," Steve pontificated, holding the lapels of his jacket in a professorial way, "was the shining truth that teachers who get on with their cleaners are naturally good teachers."

"Mrs Thompson is a lamb," Abbie told him as she added more china to the table and put the kettle on. She looked at him, suddenly serious. "In fact I love Linstowel, Steve. I just realised it. I am being healed here—" She thought of Daniel and added soberly, "Sometimes the process has hurt considerably. Nevertheless I talk about Mark and Chris—I even think about them—without any sadness. Just gratitude that I knew them and they made me what I am."

"Abbie—" Steve tried to take her hands but they were full of plates and she laughed.

"It's just little things, Steve. Like tea by the fire and Rita Lampton bossing her group about, and Lady Margaret very solemnly showing Stan Berrows how to thread a needle and Mrs Dawes refusing to pull up weeds in her garden."

There was a sudden pounding at the door and Abbie smiled.

"That'll be the twins. Trying to show us that they are well in control of the situation. Just as well they've arrived—we're getting much too serious."

Paul and Peter had obviously been given the treatment by either Tammy or their grandmother. Their hair was slicked across their foreheads and they wore identical green jerseys and fairly respectable jeans. They looked angelic.

"Come in, boys." Abbie did not let the smile in her eyes reach her mouth. "The Inspector is here to see you."

It was pathetic to watch the change in them. They had arrived defiantly, anticipating a quiet talk with their teacher, at the worst a cold admonition. What else could she do? And now, here by the familiar fireside was what amounted to the law! Peter immediately got behind Paul and Paul's swagger faded into fidgets. He put his hands in his pockets and withered.

"Tammy never said—" he began, standing just inside the sitting-room door almost on Peter's feet.

Abbie passed him and sat down opposite Steve.

"How long did you think you were going to get away with it?" she asked curtly.

"We didn't mean to stay away again. Not yesterday. We wanted to come really."

Steve stood up. "Why didn't you then?" He went to the window and looked out at the red sun sinking towards the distant sea. "You know all children between the ages of five and sixteen go to school?"

Paul ducked his head.

"You don't like school?"

Peter spoke up suddenly. "We like it. We like it very much."

"You don't like *this* school then? You would prefer Castle Combe?"

Both boys spoke together, "No!"

There was a silence. At last Steve turned very quietly and faced the two small figures.

135

"Well, why skip it?"

Paul's face was brick red and he was obviously near tears. It was Peter who crept out from behind him and went to stand by Abbie. He put his hand very gently on the sleeve of her new dress as if to feel the material.

"*You* know why. If we're not at school our Dad's got to come back home and look for us. In the end he would. If we stayed away long enough." He looked pleadingly up at her. "Wouldn't he, Mrs Eliot?"

"Of course he would, Peter," she replied gently. "But he's got troubles at the moment and he is trusting you to get on without him for a while."

"He doesn't care about us. We went down in the cove and all, but he didn't come looking."

"What rubbish. If you really believed that there'd be no point in skipping school anyway. He's just very busy."

Steve went on levelly, "In any case you know you must come to school. This school or another one. It's up to you."

Suddenly Abbie did not want Steve to tell them they might be moved. Instinct told her that if the twins thought they might lose their school it would be their last security gone. She smiled and indicated the armchair by the tea table.

"Sit down and let's have some tea, boys. You can both squeeze into that chair, can't you? I've got a rather special cake——" She didn't want them pushed into the position where they were completely defeated. If they were desperate they could do worse things than skip school. She kept talking, fetching cups and saucers and pouring them tea, making Steve comfortable.

At five o'clock she knew they would want to get home for their television programmes and she shepherded them upstairs to wash. As she saw them off she said seriously, "I want a promise from you both."

They looked at her eagerly, in a mood to promise anything.

She went on very solemnly, "It's three weeks until your half-term holiday. Not very long. Will you promise me faithfully that you will come to school until then unless your father tells you not to?"

They grinned sheepishly. Paul darted a look at Peter and said almost as cheekily as usual, "We shall have to after all that tea you ate, Peter."

Peter pretended to consider. "Okay," he said judiciously at last.

Abbie laughed. "What have I let myself in for?" she teased. "Now, seriously, boys, the next fifteen school days remember. After that I think you will come anyway. It will be too cold for beachcombing."

They ran off down the combe, chattering and laughing, all their worries temporarily forgotten. She thought urgently that she would have to overcome her diffidence, make a chance to see Daniel and tell him not to risk the boys any more.

"That promise was lightly given," Steve said behind her. "D'you think they'll keep it?"

"I don't know. What else could be done?"

She came in and shut the door. Steve was making

137

up the fire and the dim room was cosy with the flickering light. It was good to see a man there, a companionable man like Steve.

"I thought we were going to explain the position a little more explicitly to them."

"I felt quite suddenly it would be the wrong thing to do, Steve. I didn't tell you this, but I knew the father . . . before. We met him when we were on holiday two years ago, just after he had lost his wife. The boys have his wildness—the mother was by no means a quiet woman either it would seem—and I felt if we had taken away this weapon they have—truancy —they might have found a much worse one."

"Abbie, are you sure you're not dramatising this a little? What else could they do?"

She said quietly, "Their mother may well have committed suicide, Steve."

"Oh, really, my dear!"

"Yesterday, one of the managers saw the boys below the cliff from which she . . . fell. They refused to hear him when he called."

"That's what Paul meant—" he said uncomfortably. "Abbie, you didn't explain this fully to me."

"But, Steve, I know now that you were right. Paul and Peter need the village school—you heard what they said. It's the only unchanging thing in their lives. If they're taken away, or it folds up for any other reason, that's almost the last bastion—"

"You can't keep a school going for two small boys.

Nor put up with repeated truancy because you think it's a useful alternative to suicide."

"Steve, you're being unfair."

They were nearly having a row. Suddenly they both realised it and relaxed at the same time.

"Oh, Abbie—"

"Steve, I'm sorry." She was laughing rather breath-lessly. "You see how it is with me, I'm getting narrow-minded. I can think of nothing else."

"Sit down. Let's talk about—let's talk about us. What shall we do next weekend?"

He pushed two chairs together and they sat down, but the rift between them was only bridged.

"I shall be making a new set of work cards for my tinies. Practising a new hymn tune, and working out a scheme for next half term that will include an orchestrated Nativity play!"

"And then perhaps on Sunday we could drive inland. Have a meal . . ." he began persuasively. He picked up her hand and held it lightly between the chair.

"Steve," she frowned, searching for tactful words. "You—you wouldn't get too serious about our friend-ship—would you? I mean, I couldn't monopolise your time—"

"Oh, Abbie. You must know how I feel about you."

She pulled her hand free and stood up, suddenly agitated.

"You hardly know me."

There was a tap at the front door which they both ignored.

139

"I know all I need to know, my dear." He stood up to face her. He was very close and she could smell the fresh-linen smell of his shirt. She tried to step back, but the hearth was right behind her. "I think, in our four meetings, we both know each other pretty well."

"Steve, please. Don't rush anything. I really am years older than you—"

"I'm not rushing you, Abbie. I just want you to think of me—well, in a special way. Don't turn your head, my dear. I realise that in your heart you are still married to your Mark. All I ask is that you let me see you. Let me try to find a place for myself in your life."

His clever eyes were pleading and she felt her own soften in sympathy. His arms were gentle on her shoulders and she knew it would indeed be cruel to turn away now.

As his lips met hers the kitchen door opened and over his shoulder she saw Daniel standing there. He wore the deep red jersey she had chosen for him last week in Casterbridge and it emphasised his darkness.

She jerked away from Steve convulsively and somehow stepped around him.

"Daniel—" It sounded like an excuse and she stopped herself.

"It's okay, Abbie. I'm sorry. I didn't realise . . ."

They stood there like puppets, apparently unable to move.

He said at last, "I did knock, but you didn't answer, yet I could see the kitchen light was on. I was worried."

Steve moved and broke the spell. Trying to reduce

the situation to normal, he said casually, "This is Mr Enys?"

"Yes." Abbie wished he hadn't said that. It might look as if they had been discussing Daniel. "Stephen Bennett, the Schools Adviser for the County," she introduced him formally.

"Quite," Daniel said dryly. "I'd better go." He turned and went back through the kitchen and Abbie followed him.

"Daniel, there must have been something—what did you want?"

He paused in the open doorway. It was quite dark outside and the bare apple tree shook a few leaves over the garden path making the still frosty night seem colder than it really was. She shivered.

"Go on inside, Abbie. I only came to tell you I took Margo to catch the midday train today. So I can keep a better eye on the boys. There'll be no more truancy."

He was gone. Abbie hung on to the door staring after him and thinking what a waste of time it had all been today after all. If she hadn't gone into Casterbridge and Steve hadn't come home with her, Daniel might have stayed and talked and told her about Ghislaine . . .

Steve was behind her and she closed the door and turned to him as naturally as she could.

He stared at her flushed face.

"You didn't tell me everything by any means, did you, Abbie?"

"Steve, please. I'm very tired."

"It's all right, my dear. I won't pester you any more

141

with my unwelcome attentions." He picked up the hairy jacket from the back of a chair and pushed his arms into it. "It seems as if the problem of the Enys boy has been solved without my help—or your worrying, Abbie."

She couldn't explain any more, and anyway what was there to explain? Suddenly it all seemed futile and hopeless and she was bone-tired. Last night she had wondered if Daniel might be a murderer, but at least there had been some kind of understanding between them. Now . . . she could imagine what the intimate scene between herself and Steve had looked like from the kitchen door. Colour washed through her face and she wanted to cry from sheer frustration.

"Good night, Abbie." He turned on the steps leading down to the combe road where his car was parked. If she could have found the strength to lean forward and kiss his cheek, the breach might have been partially healed. But she couldn't.

"Good night, Steve," she said.

She watched while he switched on his lights and drove away. She had a feeling she wouldn't be seeing him for a while.

Nor Daniel.

Tears trickled down her face.

SEVEN

DURING the following weeks Abbie proved yet again that by immersing herself in day-to-day affairs she could push larger worries to the back of her mind. Now that the immediacy of her difficulties with Paul and Peter were postponed, she plunged back into school life with a sense of relief though she knew that her normal, tidy, school life was only temporary.

The difference in the boys was striking. It caused Abbie to look back over Miss Liddell's records for the previous year and note down her comments on their behaviour. Although the boys had few favourable remarks to their credit, there seemed to be four really bad patches when, according to Miss Liddell, they were "almost unmanageable". Abbie took careful note of the dates. If she got chance to talk to Daniel and could check that these were the times that Margo had been visiting Linstowel, it might prove useful ammunition in any kind of plea she might be able to make on behalf of the boys.

Meanwhile Daniel met them most evenings and they were full of stories of fishing trips and smoky bonfires on the damp beach. Mrs Enys called at the school house the next weekend and asked Abbie to forget her out-burst.

"If only Margo will stay away, Abbie, I can tell myself that the kind of thing I said to you the other evening is ridiculous—" She managed a little laugh. "It is, isn't it, my dear? Daniel could never do such a terrible thing—"

"I told you last Saturday, put it out of your mind. The police would have followed it up. But in any case if there had been a—terrible accident—Daniel would have told them himself."

But even as she said it, a question rose unbidden to Abbie's mind. What if there had been some kind of struggle before Ghislaine fell to her death; might Daniel have kept silent for the sake of his sons?

But it reassured Mrs Enys and, like Abbie, she was willing to push the problem away from her for a time and enjoy this period of calm with her little family.

The school seemed a very lively place these days. Mr Dawes came on a Wednesday afternoon with his records and took the top group for French. Lady Margaret still came on Tuesdays and Thursdays and was staying on in the afternoons for various reasons. She went for a long walk with the tinies one day and they came back with nearly four pounds of blackberries for bramble jelly. Abbie herself, besides making certain the whole school took it in turns in her kitchen to try their hands at cooking—and to write about it afterwards—started her recorder group and introduced them into the morning prayers. Several mothers came to see her after school to ask if they could buy recorders for their children. She began to discuss a possible carol concert with the children and set the middle group to making simple percussion instruments.

Her greatest joy came on the day they broke up for half term. The children were standing ready in their crocodile to walk across the playground to their mothers and Abbie was checking that every glove and dap was out of the cloakroom to give Mrs Thompson chance for a really good clean. The children looked angelic, their faces beaming with the prospect of a whole week to themselves, their arms full of treasured pictures and models they were allowed to take home with them. They chattered in low voices as Abbie pulled on a forgotten hat and tied a hanging shoe-lace. Then they were silent as a young woman appeared in the doorway, pushing a pushchair containing a toddler and with a small, plump four-year-old clutching the handle.

"It's the doctor's wife, Mrs Eliot," announced Rita Lampton importantly. "She must have left her new baby at home. Or—" she looked eagerly at the smiling face, "—in the car?"

The newcomer laughed. "Yes, I'm Mrs Wiley." She looked at Abbie. "And if Mrs Eliot doesn't mind, you may look in the car on your way out. The new baby— by the way her name is Clare—is asleep in the carry-cot, so please don't wake her."

Abbie shook hands with Mrs Wiley and stood by the door until the children were safely out of the playground. Mrs Enys had told her the young doctor's wife was expecting another baby and was staying with her mother at Castle Combe, and Abbie wondered if this was just a social visit.

Mrs Wiley was walking around the denuded school-room.

"My dear, everywhere Bart visits he is told what a wonderful job you're doing here—" Abbie guessed that Bart must be Doctor Wiley. She tried to explain that most of the display work had been taken down for half term.

"Yes, but I can see how well you've planned everything. Look, Meg—you can sit on the cushions here and read all these lovely books—do you mind, Mrs Eliot? Just while we talk."

"Not at all," said Abbie. "Won't you sit down at my desk—or perhaps you'd like a cup of tea over at the house?"

Mrs Wiley shook her head. "No, thanks. I'm in a shocking hurry as usual—I wanted to come earlier and see how you worked. Perhaps I could after the holiday?"

Abbie hesitated. Casual visitors, especially visitors with small children, could be distracting.

"We might be able to arrange something," she said cautiously. "Was there anything particular you were interested in?"

"Not really. It's just that if you could take Meg after Christmas—she'll be five in January—it would be rather nice if she could come in for half-an-hour once or twice and get the feel of . . . well, school!"

"Oh, of course!" That was quite different. Any sensible teacher welcomed this kind of approach to school life. "I'm simply delighted you're considering sending Meg to this school, Mrs Wiley. You doubtless realise the situation in Linstowel, every new pupil helps to keep the school open."

Mrs Wiley gave her open smile again. "Well, I think every parent must prefer to send their children to a local school and when they hear such terrific reports—"

Abbie laughed. "Stop it, Mrs Wiley—"

"No, seriously—"

Abbie turned to Meg to hide her embarrassment, but she was delighted with this new turn of events.

Before she left, Mrs Wiley asked her to come to dinner the following Wednesday.

"I've been out of things for much too long," she said wryly. "I've lived just outside Linstowel for six years now, yet I only know people through my husband—my social life is still at home in Castle Combe. It's because of all the babies, of course, there's been no time for entertaining. So I'm turning over a new leaf. A dinner party next Wednesday—I'm a rotten cook, I'm warning you—but you'll meet—" she waved a dramatic hand, "—Everybody!" She chuckled richly. "That means the Lamptons, the Dawes, Lady Margaret, Dan Enys, Mrs Filbert, Jenny Berrows—"

"I thought you didn't know anyone!" said Abbie.

"I went to school with Dan and the Filberts and Jenny Berrows," Mrs Wiley grinned. "It's the others that petrify me. And you, of course."

Abbie laughed again. She realised it would be hopeless to take this girl seriously. She was much too young to have gone to school with Daniel, even though she probably knew the others from schooldays. Abbie glanced at her sharply. Might she be trying her hand at a little matchmaking?

"Your husband has been doctoring the whole of Linstowel for the past six years then?" she asked casually as she walked across the deserted playground with her visitor.

"Except for his time off, when the Castle Combe man stands in. It's not a big village and everyone keeps fairly healthy, so it isn't as tough as it sounds."

Abbie waved goodbye thoughtfully. She had accepted Mrs Wiley's dinner invitation gratefully because it promised to lighten a rather dull week's holiday. But there were other reasons as well. It might be the means of talking to Daniel calmly and reasonably—though it was impossible to imagine talking to Daniel with any degree of calmness. And it might be an opportunity of finding out something about Ghislaine from another source: her doctor.

On Sunday she went to church to hear Mr Dawes preach and was quietly pleased to see Daniel and the boys sitting in a front pew. They all spoke to her on the way out and Peter delved in his trouser pocket to show her a new shell he had found on one of their recent expeditions.

Daniel said quietly, "I can see a difference in them, Abbie. Thank you."

She looked him in the eye. "They need you, Daniel. That's why you can see a difference. Because they've got you."

He smiled slightly, "Poor little devils . . ."

Before Abbie could think about that, Paul was demanding as loudly as ever that she come to tea.

"Tammy let us make some of your scones, Mrs Eliot," he boasted. "Better than those Job Wyatt and Matthew Filbert made. D'you want to come and taste them?"

"Well . . ." Abbie said doubtfully. Daniel said nothing, but he still smiled and his one eyebrow asked a question. "I don't know whether it would be convenient."

"Perfectly convenient with us," Daniel said. "It depends on your friend perhaps?" At her slight frown he added, "The School Adviser of course."

She flushed brightly. She had managed to push all thoughts of Steve to the back of her mind with the bigger problem of Daniel, and the sudden reminder of that unfortunate scene in her sitting-room three weeks ago made her flinch with embarrassment.

She said as calmly as she could, "Naturally, Mr Bennett has not called on me again—" It occurred to her suddenly that neither had the library van, and she had heard nothing of any museum exhibits either. Surely Steve wouldn't extract such petty revenge for her lack of response that evening? Suddenly she made up her mind, "I should like to come to tea, Paul. Thank you for asking me."

Did she imagine Daniel's pleasure? He said quickly, before she could change her mind, "We'll call for you, shall we, boys? About three."

They arrived at quarter to three just before she could change her dress for the second time. She had wondered whether the brown wool with the lemon scarf was a bit too obviously "Sunday-best", but there was no time to change again or pin her hair into its normal severe style. Feeling rather stupidly frivolous, she slipped into an old tweed coat by way of toning herself down, and locked the front door before she could glimpse herself again in the mirror. Paul noticed immediately of course.

"Your hair's all long and fluffy, Mrs Eliot," he announced loudly as she got into the old Morris next to Daniel—the boys took up the back seat. "It's nice like that. Like a dandelion clock."

"You did know your son was a budding poet," Abbie said dryly to Daniel as she settled herself. "Seriously he has got a definite literary bent. His stories and poems are very imaginative."

Daniel replied equally dryly, "So I've noticed."

Peter put in more quietly as her coat fell open, "I like that dress, too. It's got a nice soft feel."

Daniel caught her eye and smiled. Abbit felt immediately the link between them. "No good standing on ceremony with children is there?" he asked quietly.

She turned and smiled at the boys. It was true the children—these and the others at school—were her salvation. Their naturalness had a healing power even when it hurt. In an odd way, their naturalness was like

Daniel's. It was at least real, it had no social veneer to poison it. With the boys chattering in the back seat, the strong pull of her strange relationship with their father became something normal and not to be feared. She wondered how she could have imagined, even for a fleeting second, that Daniel could have killed anyone. What was more incredible perhaps was that he could risk the happiness of his sons by his inexplicable allegiance to the wayward Margo Ritchie. There was so much to be explained, but once again, she decided to postpone her worries.

It was a happy afternoon, the sort of afternoon she had known from, what seemed now, like another life. Paul was still occasionally obstreperous, but Peter was much gentler and his quiet smile was a reflection of his father's.

The clocks had gone back and the evening closed in early while they were walking along the cliff looking for the last of the late blackberries. They clambered muddily back into the car and sang one of the songs from school while Daniel drove back to the Lobster Pot and the enormous high tea Tammy had prepared for them in the little room overlooking the harbour. After hot scones, dripping with butter, Abbie played the piano and Daniel strummed on his guitar, while they all sang together until Tammy announced the boys' bed-time.

"I must go," Abbie said, suddenly startled out of her family mood at the prospect of being alone with Daniel.

She made her thanks to the boys and to Tammy, who

kept telling her she should come more often. And then she was with Daniel in the old Morris, knowing that if she put off her talk with him any longer, it would be from sheer self-indulgence.

"Janet Wiley tells me you'll be at her dinner party next Wednesday, Abbie," Daniel said as they drew up at the school house. They had been talking about Paul's unexpectedly musical voice, and the sudden change of subject seemed almost like an opening.

"Yes." Abbie laughed. "She told me you would be there too. And that you and she were at school together."

"We both attended Casterbridge. But hardly at the same time. I've a feeling Janet Wiley is living up to her name."

"Perhaps. Will you go?"

"I wasn't going to." She felt his eyes on her in the darkness. "Abbie, I've enjoyed this afternoon. But you must know that it cannot lead to anything else."

Her mouth was dry and she felt stifled. "Daniel, please don't . . . speak to me . . . as you did before. I couldn't bear it again. I promise you I have no . . . designs on you—" She tried a laugh, but it sounded more like a gasp. "I might have wondered—perhaps I still wonder—whether we couldn't be friends . . ."

"Maybe." Suddenly his warm hand closed over her cold one. "Though it is hard to imagine, feeling as we both do."

"Daniel—"

"Oh, Abbie, at least let us be honest. We could be much more than friends. Don't forget I know the real

Abigail Eliot. I knew you with Mark and Christopher, so I know the whole of you. Not the tiny bit your—School Adviser—thinks he knows."

"That was—a mistake. I *could* be friends with Steve. Nothing else."

He gripped her hand. "I know. And you need a friend. Especially someone like that, in authority. Why don't you telephone him and make it up—"

"How can you talk like that? How can we be sitting here talking about Steve when there is so much more we have to discuss? Daniel, just tell me, is the reason why we cannot be . . . friends . . . something to do with Margo Ritchie?"

He laughed shortly and let go of her hand. "Obviously. But not the way you think. Margo is ill. She comes to the cottage occasionally for a cure. I have to be with her all the time, Abbie, but believe me, I am merely a—nurse, if you like."

There was a short silence, then Abbie said in a low voice, "Is she an alcoholic, Daniel?"

"Yes, my dear," he replied wearily. "What's more to the point I suppose—so was my wife."

"Oh, Daniel. I'm so sorry."

"I didn't know it at the time, of course, otherwise I'd have called in Doc Wiley. Apparently, according to Margo, she went to a doctor privately. In London. So she must have realised she was sick. I don't want to bore you with details, Abbie. But on the night of her death Ghislaine and I had our final row. She went off to the cottage and got roaring drunk and on her way back

153

home to try to make some kind of reconciliation, she fell off the cliff."

"Daniel, how do you know this?"

"I didn't, not at first. I didn't know it when you were here on holiday. I felt frightful, of course, but as far as I knew Ghislaine had had a terrible accident anyone might have had, and it was my duty to remember the good times and forget the bad. Then Margo rolled up and informed me she had been at the cottage that night. Ghislaine had arrived there bitterly unhappy about our marriage—genuinely anxious for the first time, to make a go of it for the sake of the children. She tried to find some Dutch courage. Margo heard her screaming as she fell."

"Oh, my God."

"Quite. Margo cleared off, but it didn't improve her condition." He was quiet and she stole a glance at his profile in the dim light from the dashboard. It was iron-hard.

He said flatly, "She promised she'd keep it quiet if I let her use the cottage when she was . . . ill. I'm not being blackmailed, Abbie—don't think that. I try to look after Margo from common humanity, and for the sake of Ghislaine. I didn't look after *her* very well, did I?"

"Daniel, you can't reproach yourself for something you didn't even know about—"

He laughed shortly. "Now you're trying to tell me I do it from guilt motives. Perhaps you're right. I don't know any more. I keep telling Margo she'll have to get proper treatment and then she pulls herself together and I really think she's improving. When she rolls up again she's usually bitter and says some rotten things about the way I ignored Ghislaine, and I imagine her saying that kind of thing to the boys . . . or to that idiot Lampton . . ."

Abbie shuddered.

"I can see how it is," she agreed at last. "But I refuse to look on it as a closed situation. There must be something to be done. I'll talk to Margo—try to get her to go to hospital—"

"How will that change things, Abbie? Nothing anyone can do will change the real situation. When it comes to it the village gossip isn't so far from the real truth, is it? I am responsible for my wife's death. The only thing I can hope to salvage from the whole wretched affair is Peter and Paul's trust. If they hear their mother was an alcoholic and fell over the cliff after I'd practically driven her out of the house . . . where does that get us? Besides, the intervals between Margo's . . . visits are getting longer. She didn't come between April and September."

"And before that it was February, then just before Christmas and again in October?"

"How did you know that?"

"Those were the times when Miss Liddell wrote in her records Paul and Peter were 'unmanageable'. You might be saving them in one way, Daniel, but you're sacrificing them in another."

"Abbie, stop making it more difficult. They've got

155

Tammy and my mother can stand in for me now. Besides . . . maybe Margo is permanently cured now."

"Maybe . . ." Abbie sighed sharply. Even if Margo were cured—and this she very much doubted—it seemed as though Daniel would be a man haunted by his past for a long time to come.

"We've talked long enough," Daniel said quickly. "I didn't want to burden you, Abbie, but you've been so good. And anyway I felt I owed you an explanation. There's no point in examining the feeling between us, my dear, but in the circumstances it cannot bring us happiness." He got out of the car abruptly and came round to open the door for her. "You know where I am if I can do anything." He helped her up the steps to her front door. "Good night, Abbie. Sleep well, my dear." His mouth brushed her cheek and she turned instinctively towards him, but he was gone. He moved lightly for such a big man and she heard nothing more until the car door slammed, and immediately afterwards the engine sprang into life. Only as his tail-light disappeared around the bend did she unlock the door and go back into her little cottage. And then for a long time she sat without taking off her coat, gazing at her carefully stacked fire, thinking, not of Daniel's insoluble difficulties, but of Daniel himself. Impulsive, almost wild, but warmly alive and endearingly human.

The night of Janet Wiley's dinner party was cold and frosty with the sky full of stars. Abbie had been for a long walk in the afternoon past Margo Ritchie's cottage and down into the little cove. The sea had been grey and sullen with hardly a ripple to disturb its metallic stillness. The thought of Paul and Peter clambering down here to try to shock their father back home was disturbing. She could only hope that Margo was permanently cured. She went home to drink a cup of tea and bathe and change with a curious feeling of something about to happen. It must be the frosty weather, she decided, as, with a sigh, she once again slipped into her russet-brown frock. There was no reason for her anticipation as Daniel was not to be at the party—and in any case after their talk the other evening she was a fool to hope for another chance to be with him . . . she sighed again. She was a fool indeed.

If she had half-hoped he would change his mind and come to the party, she was disappointed. Mr Dawes picked her up at six-thirty and drove her along the Castle Combe road to a red brick family house about two miles from the village. Mary Dawes was dressed for the occasion in a long wool skirt and frilly top and informed Abbie she had had to threaten Arnold with starvation if he didn't come. "He wouldn't have come for my sake, dear," she said brazenly. "But when I pointed out that if he didn't take the car, not only would I have to stay at home, but so would you, well, he changed his mind." Abbie giggled as she always did at this husband and wife duo. "He telephoned Mr Enys, too, and offered him a lift to save him getting out that ancient old Morris of his, but unfortunately he couldn't come." Mary Dawes glanced at Abbie and away. "We felt it only friendly to make the offer, my dear, but after that little contretemps last August, perhaps it's as well he's staying at home."

"Oh, that was just a misunderstanding," Abbie said firmly. "Mr Enys and I have had several chats—about the boys of course—and we are on good terms now."

"I'm so glad," said Mary Dawes vaguely.

The Wileys' house was warm and friendly and full of children's things; the baby's pram in the hall, a truck full of wooden bricks and a tricycle in the downstairs cloakroom. Janet and her mother took it in turns to meet the demands of either the kitchen or the children upstairs, while the guests congregated in the comfortable sitting-room and chatted over their drinks.

Doctor Wiley turned out to be a fair young man in his early thirties. He reminded Abbey strongly of Steve Bennett. He was definite and concise in his speech with that air of authority Steve possessed and which must be so reassuring to his patients.

"I shall be meeting you before Christmas," he told Abbie as he shook hands. "I see I'm down for a medical inspection of the school. I shall be interested to see what you're doing down there, my wife says the whole place is transformed."

"Hardly. The stove works and I've laid down an old carpet of mine . . ." Abbie laughed, deliberately playing her efforts down in case he should be disappointed. "Naturally I'm thrilled you've decided to send Meg to the local school. Might I have two other customers later on?"

"Certainly." There seemed no doubt in Bart Wiley's

mind about the efficiency of Linstowel school. "I want my kids to grow up with the local kids. They won't do that if I send them off to Castle Combe."

"I wish more people felt like that," Abbie commented.

"They will. You know Mr Bennett, I believe, the new School Adviser?"

"Why, yes. He's been to school once or twice actually."

"I was at County Hall last week—about the medical inspection—and we lunched together. He can't speak highly enough of you. That's the kind of advertising you need."

"I see." So Steve had lunched with Bart Wiley last week and straightaway Janet Wiley had come down to the school to see for herself. . . . It was good of Steve not to let personal feelings influence him. She would take Daniel's advice and telephone him about the library van . . . she could suggest a friendship, perhaps . . .

Janet's mother announced dinner and they all trooped into the family living-room and an enormous table beautifully laid with red and white napkins and the last of the roses from the Wiley's garden. It was a festive meal, ten of them, with Jenny Berrows and Abbie extra women—but nobody worried about that. Abbie was amused to see Stan had inherited his mother's shock of red hair together with her open, forthright manner. Because of this, she felt she knew Mrs Berrows already and they had a delightful talk over the soup. Then Abbie turned to her other neighbour, Mark Filbert, who had been the Station Master until Linstowel was turned into

159

a halt. Now he travelled daily into Casterbridge to work and already regretted the certainty that Miles and Matthew would have to do the same.

"If only we could bring tourists in," he mourned to Abbie, "Or even get a little light industry going. It would be worth putting up with housing estates and a small factory to save the village."

Abbie felt her personal triumph at the school fade a little in the light of Mr Filbert's longer-term view. Perhaps in many ways it would have been better had the school closed when Miss Liddell left. In the end, it seemed inevitable it would have to go.

They went back to the lounge for coffee and Mr Lampton wasted no time in bringing his sister-in-law over to introduce her to Abbie. This was Rita's mother, a bony woman, with the round open face Abbie would have expected. A woman who would be interested in her neighbours' doings, and who would no doubt pass on her gleanings to her brother-in-law.

She questioned Abbie avidly about Rita's progress. It was nice to be able to give whole-hearted praise.

"Rita is so sensible. She has been of endless help to me since I came to the school," Abbie concluded. "Besides which she is such a likeable little girl."

Mrs Lampton's eyes filled with tears. "It's good to hear you say that, Mrs Eliot. I expect you know I lost my husband when Rita was just a baby. Charlie's good to us—more than good, of course. But I do miss a proper father for Rita. You can understand that."

"Yes," said Abbie.

"People think we ought to get married and make a proper home together. I'd be more than willing. But Charlie will never get over Mrs Enys. He's never been the same since the night she died." The homely face looked suddenly tragic. "I remember what he said then and he meant it, too."

Abbie looked over the smooth brown hair to where Lampton was nodding his fierce weatherbeaten head at something Janet Wiley was saying. She was suddenly curious. "What did he say, Mrs Lampton?"

"Oh, it was nothing much, I suppose. Not when you repeat it. It was the way he said it, Mrs Eliot. As if he was making a vow almost. He said, 'I might have forgotten her if she'd lived—one day, but now she's dead, I'll never forget her, not as long as I have breath in my body'. It was a queer thing to say straight after he found her body, wasn't it?"

"Mr Lampton found her body?" said Abbie.

"Yes. I thought he might have told you. He can't stop talking about it. It shocked him. Of course, that cottage belonged to him and he often walks along to the cove. Even now. It made him morbid, Mrs Eliot."

Abbie looked into the wide, frank eyes, so like Rita's.

"Yes," she agreed. "Perhaps it did. He has mentioned Mrs Enys to me several times. I'm afraid I've been—unsympathetic."

So she had been right. Lampton had been in love with Ghislaine Enys; might even have been the man who caused Daniel to threaten her life. And he had discovered her body. That meant that Margo and Lampton had been on the scene. Did either of them know that the other one was there?

Before she left, Abbie arranged another tête-a-tête with Bart Wiley. There was something else she badly wanted to know.

"I intended talking to you about Ghislaine Enys tonight, Doctor," she began frankly as she took her empty coffee cup into the kitchen. "I have a little difficulty with the Enys twins and I wondered if there was something you might know about their mother that could possibly help me."

"Of course, anything I can do to help. But I hardly knew Ghislaine. I delivered the twins—she was disgustingly healthy; they came too soon as easily as possible— but then she went into Casterbridge hospital, and after that I suppose I saw her once or twice when they were little. There was never anything wrong with her."

"Did you do the post mortem after the accident?"

He looked surprised. "My dear, there wasn't one. The cause of death was obvious. She was terribly battered, of course."

"I see. There is talk in the village of . . . a struggle. I wondered if her body was marked in any way."

"Ah. The gossip is affecting the children, I suppose. What a terrible pity. No way of scotching it either. It would have taken someone far more expert than myself to detect any signs of a struggle. And of course she was cremated at Casterbridge."

"Oh." Abbie felt deflated. She had been so certain she was on the track of . . . something. "I'm sorry to bother you, Doctor. I just hoped to hear something that would stop the gossip once and for all." Even the charge of alcoholism came from Margo's lips only. Unless, of course, Lampton knew about it.

"I'm only too glad to help, Mrs Eliot. Any kind of background information I might have about the children—please telephone me any time. I realise without some kind of thumbnail sketch and family backgrounds, you're often working entirely in the dark."

Abbie smiled her gratitude, but she felt absurdly disappointed. Naturally, if Ghislaine had been visiting a London doctor privately, Doctor Wiley would probably have no idea of her condition on the night of the accident, yet it seemed incredible that no one except Margo had realised her true illness. There was, after all, quite a difference between being . . . gay . . . and being a true alcoholic. Was it possible Margo was exaggerating Ghislaine's liking for a "good time" into something that would increase Daniel's hurt, his sense of responsibility?

The Dawes were fetching their coats and Abbie signalled to them that she was just coming. Mary hurried over to enquire whether she would mind waiting while Arnold took Mrs Berrows and Mrs Lampton down to the village first.

"I've got a headache, my dear—nothing to worry about, I do assure you. But I'd like Arnold to take me back first if you really don't mind waiting."

Lampton was helping his sister-in-law with her coat and Abbie wondered at his lack of chivalry in leaving her with the Dawes when he had presumably brought her. Then it transpired he had actually walked the two miles here and was proposing to walk back. Abbie was struck by an idea.

"I'll walk with you, Mr Lampton," she said quickly. "It will save Mr Dawes coming back for me and it's just the night for a walk. I'm sure you won't mind company."

He turned his usual puce colour. "Not at all, Mrs Eliot. I agree it's grand weather for walking and we've a lot to talk over."

Abbie slid her arms into the coat he held for her. "Yes," she said thoughtfully.

Arnold Dawes protested of course, but Abbie was adamant, and after profuse thanks to the Wileys she and Lampton set off at a brisk pace down the Castle Combe road. Probably because of their past searing frankness, there was an ease between them which Abbie had not appreciated before. She could expect no polite small talk from Lampton, and need not therefore make any herself. They were silent as they walked downhill towards the dark sea which glimmered in the distance under the stars.

"It's beautiful, isn't it?" Abbie said at last. "I can understand you wanting to keep the village alive. Though in one way perhaps you should be one of those to leave it behind."

He was startled. "Why?"

She said deliberately, "To forget Ghislaine Enys."

He was speechless for a long moment, then he said, "My sister-in-law talking again, I suppose. She doesn't understand, of course. Thinks I'm in love with a dream."

Abbie wanted to say—poor Charlie Lampton . . . but she said nothing. They walked on impassively, presumably Lampton wrapped in his dream, Abbie wondering how to break it.

Eventually she said bluntly, "Can you tell me, Mr Lampton, was Ghislaine an alcoholic?"

He stopped suddenly so that she left him behind a few paces. "Who told you that?" he demanded fiercely. Then, when she didn't immediately answer, it seemed as if he forced himself to walk on and speak normally. "Whoever it was spoke the truth. Yes, she was an alcoholic. She was drunk when she went over the cliff that night. She'd have never gone otherwise. She knew every inch of the coastline and she was as sure-footed as a mule." He hesitated, then added, "And about as stubborn."

Abbie walked on silently. So Daniel had been right and Margo was speaking the truth. There were no hidden facts after all. She knew she could trust Lampton to speak the truth. He might have wanted to lie to protect his "dream", it seemed as if he almost had, but then his natural blunt honesty had taken over.

It seemed as though Daniel might well be haunted for ever by the vision of his remorseful wife falling over the cliff in a drunken stupor.

EIGHT

THE weeks flew by towards Christmas. Watching the progress made by Paul and Peter Enys, Abbie began to feel that Daniel's overwhelming remorse might well be healed by time. He was often in the shop helping his mother and she told Abbie over tea that he was considering opening his guest-rooms again next season.

The other children in the school, too, were progressing in leaps and bounds. Abbie was often touched by their terrific enthusiasm, the way they brought bits and pieces from home to show her. It was proof that the knowledge she gave them during school was being put to good use outside.

Janet Wiley brought Meg in for two afternoons and told Abbie privately that one of Bart's patients whose children attended Castle Combe Primary School was considering moving them lock, stock and barrel to Linstowel. This would increase the numbers by four after the Christmas term. She made this bit of news an excuse to telephone Steve one evening and make a move to heal the breach between them.

It was obvious she had been on his mind a great deal.

"Abbie, I didn't know what to do. You must have thought me incredibly brash and stupid. I suppose I was carried away by the suddenness of our friendship. I've picked up the phone several times and put it down—"

"Steve, stop making mountains out of molehills. And thanks for fixing the library van—and the marvellous Roman coin collection."

"Is it helping?"

"Marilyn Thompson buried some old pennies under my apple tree for future generations to find. Does that answer the question?"

He laughed. "Could we meet occasionally, Abbie? See a film—talk. I promise I'll be very sensible."

"Of course. But I don't want to monopolise you. I want you to meet a nice girl—Steve, stop laughing, I mean it!"

"You and my mother both. All right. I'll keep looking. Meanwhile, will you come into Casterbridge on the eleven o'clock and have lunch with me next Saturday?"

She went and thoroughly enjoyed herself. Steve wanted to drive her home but she was adamant that she would go on the train.

"For you to drive sixty miles on my behalf is exactly what I meant about monopolising you," she explained severely. "No, I am not worried that in the comfort of the school house you will—forget yourself—again—" He was laughing uproariously at what he called her "teacher manner". "It's just that during the two or three hours you were with me, you could be—"

He interrupted dramatically, "Looking around!"

"Exactly," she said primly.

As it happened she had company on the train. Lady Margaret was on the platform and they travelled back together, hardly talking because of the rattle of the coaches, but as quietly companionable as they always were. It occurred to Abbie once or twice that Lady Margaret was looking her age. She leaned her head against the back of the seat in a weary way that Abbie had never noticed before. Probably Lady Margaret had problems of her own, which Abbie knew she would never unbend enough to share. Could they be financial ones? Abbie watched as Lady Margaret drove away from the halt with her ancient cook-housekeeper who was also apparently her chauffeur. Abbie was reminded of a conversation she had had with Mrs Enys during her first days at Linstowel. It had been about Margo's painting and the fact that she saw through people's façades to their true selves—sometimes just a pile of bones. Abbie wondered what was behind Lady Margaret's façade. One thing she knew; without her stiff-necked pride—her façade—she would be nothing.

It was a pity that this superficial contentment, so hard-won for most of them, should be threatened at the beginning of December by the sudden appearance of Margo. Strange that Abbie should be the first to know of her return to the village.

It was the dinner break; half the children were playing outside in scarves and gloves against the grey winter day, the other half were sitting around the stove, reading or playing table games while Abbie sat at her desk marking books. The dinner lady came through the cloakroom

168

and called to Abbie that a visitor was knocking on the
school house door and should she show her up to the
school.

"No, thank you, Mrs Davis. I'm going over for coffee
anyway." She issued her usual warnings about the stove
and slipped her coat over her shoulders. It was good to
know she could trust the children inside the school alone.
Any of the top two groups were now quite capable of
dealing with the needs of the tinies and showed a
thoughtfulness and consideration towards each other that
made Abbie feel personally proud of them.

This feeling of order was completely shattered by the
sight of Margo, practically hanging on to her front door,
her head against the jamb, her whole body shaking
convulsively.

"Miss Ritchie!" Abbie ran forward and put an arm
around the thin shoulders. How suddenly evident it was
that Margo's condition was true illness. Daniel ought
never to be trying to cope with this alone. "Lean on me,
my dear. Let me just get the key into the door—"

Unexpectedly Margo stiffened herself and stood erect.

"Don't fuss. I'm absolutely all right. Travelled all
night and simply exhausted . . ."

She walked steadily into the sitting-room and then
crumpled up like a collapsed puppet on to the nearest
chair.

"I'm so cold," she moaned. "So cold . . ."

The fire was laid for the end of afternoon school and
Abbie put a match to it and then plugged in the electric

169

bowl fire and trained it on to the shivering figure. Margo began to weep softly like a child, but immediately Abbie tried to comfort her she shrugged herself angrily away and for a few moments held herself upright before her next collapse. Frantically Abbie made black coffee. She had no idea how to treat Margo. Her one coherent thought was . . . poor Daniel.

After a lot of persuasion she managed to get Margo to drink some of the coffee. The room was warming up quickly and already the unkempt head was lolling back uncomfortably into sleep. There was no sofa in the small sitting-room, so in desperation Abbie piled cushions in front of the fire and somehow lugged Margo's almost inert body on to them. Then she covered her with a blanket, switched off the electric fire, fixed the guard securely in front of the coal fire and ran back across the playground to school, suddenly frantic in case anyone should find out. What on earth could she do? She was very reluctant to call Daniel in, yet there seemed no alternative. Margo in her present state would surely talk her head off when she came round, and after all Daniel had been through to keep her secret from the boys . . . Then she thought of Lampton. He knew already that Ghislaine had been an alcoholic and he had his own romantic reasons for keeping the knowledge to himself. Perhaps he could help out. If they could just get Margo over this bout. . . . Abbie realised she must be thinking as Daniel had so often thought.

Never had three-thirty taken so long to arrive. At last the children were gone and Mrs Thompson was closing windows and raking out the stove. Abbie cut her short on her latest story about Janie's condition and rushed across to the school house. Margo lay as she had left her, her long hair lank across the cushions, her hands twitching on the blanket.

Abbie stepped across her and into the study. She had never been pleased to hear Lampton's voice before. Now it was a lifeline.

She told the facts quickly. They were few after all. Lampton seemed to know the rest by instinct. It occurred to Abbie, not for the first time, that there was more to Lampton than she had at first thought.

He said immediately, "Get hold of Enys. Get her up to the cottage quickly. Out of the way."

"I don't want to do that. The boys are so settled—the whole family seem to be healing—"

"They've no right to heal!" She was appalled at his malevolence. "She's got no right to be alive with Ghislaine dead! Get her out of the way."

"That's why I'm telephoning you. I know how you feel about Ghislaine and I'm terribly sorry. But Daniel can't cope with this alone much longer. It's an explosive situation for him. For you and me, it's—well, certainly not explosive. If you could have her at the farm—you're there alone—just for tonight, I can take her into Casterbridge tomorrow." Her mind was leaping ahead. Would it be unfair to ask Steve to get her into a hospital right away somewhere?

"All right." Lampton's voice was hard with sudden decision. "All right, I'll do it. Don't let anybody see her.

I don't want to be associated with any of this. It's—
it's unsavoury."

Abbie almost smiled at the typical understatement.
Then she was hurrying to rouse Margo, wash her face
and hands, try to smooth her tangled hair.

"Let me sleep—" the voice was slurred with ex-
haustion. "Don't tell Daniel. He hates me enough. Let
me sleep."

"Nobody hates you, Margo. We want to help, you
know that. Why don't you forget all the old bitterness
and go into hospital. I could arrange it very easily."

"Don't be a fool—" The heavy eyes and low flat voice
were almost amused. "Then I should have to face it all
properly, shouldn't I?"

The wintry dusk filled the room, but Abbie hesitated
to switch on any lights in case Mrs Thompson saw them
as an invitation to her usual Friday cup of tea.

She said urgently, "Margo, what do you mean? What
would you have to face? Surely everything would be
simpler if you were permanently cured?"

Margo hoisted herself up to lean back against a chair.
She shivered again. "Surely you realise by now I'm in
love with Daniel? I knew him almost before Ghislaine.
I've been in love with him for years . . ." Her eyes filled
with tears. "I know what's happening—those boys—
skipping school—my fault—" She broke down completely and at last let Abbie help her, hanging on to her
comforting arm as if she was drowning.

"Margo, listen—Mr Lampton will be here at any
minute—can you hear me—" The sobbing became more

172

controlled and Abbie hurried on. "If you really love Daniel, couldn't you think of him? You're ruining any chance of happiness he might have—"

The sobbing stopped as abruptly as it had begun and Margo pulled away.

"You're such a fool, Mrs Eliot—such a sheltered fool! If you'd known Ghislaine, perhaps you'd understand. Everyone loved her—Daniel, Charlie Lampton, even that old fool Dawes. Someone killed her that night, but we're all responsible. There'll be no—happiness—for any of us—"

"What do you mean, someone killed her?" Abbie gripped the thin shoulders fiercely. Margo's eyes slid away but she answered readily enough.

"I heard her screaming. Over and over again. I'll never forget it—"

There was an urgent knock at the front door and Abbie ran to let in Lampton. He stood just inside the sitting-room staring at Margo's figure with unveiled disgust. Abbie peered through the kitchen and saw the school lights still on.

"You'd better stay until Mrs Thompson has left— she'll call before she goes, but if she sees you here she won't expect to come in."

"Look." Lampton followed her into the kitchen. "Why can't she stay here? I can't do anything for her— you'll have to come as well—"

"Yes, I'll come and settle her in. But you must realise she can't stay here. If she wanders out while I'm in school tomorrow—"

173

She had lowered her voice, but Margo heard and laughed her loud, hard laugh.

"I've got you all, just where I want you," she said without triumph. "I've got Daniel—I've got poor old Charlie Lampton, and now I've got the school mistress. Just like Ghislaine. But I won't let it all go to my head like Ghislaine did—"

Lampton's face was suffused with anger as he rounded on her savagely. Abbie came between them.

"Can't you see she's ill—take no notice. Here's some coffee—sit down while I pack a bag."

She ran upstairs and thrust some clothes into an overnight bag. Mrs Enys sometimes called on a Wednesday evening and Mrs Filbert was coming to sort out recorder music—Abbie felt a sense of urgency that was very near to panic. She heard Mrs Thompson come to the kitchen door and Lampton's surly voice inform her that Mrs Eliot was busy, then Margo's low hard laugh and Lampton's suddenly vicious, "Shut up!" Was it such a good idea to send Margo up to Lampton's place? She had certainly not imagined that Lampton's natural dislike could border on hatred for a friend of Ghislaine's.

She rejoined them as quickly as she could.

"Did you have a suitcase or anything, Margo?" No point in calling her Miss Ritchie any longer. "I've put a few things for you in here—"

"I walked out of my studio just as I am—" Margo seemed to be taking a perverse pleasure in all the arrangements going on around her. "I'd had enough—

174

enough—enough—" She began to weep and Lampton turned away with a snort of disgust.

"I'll take this down to the car and come back to help you with her," he said. "I suppose she can't walk."

"I can walk beautifully!" Margo pulled herself up somehow and took a few mincing steps to the fireplace. Abbie caught her before she fell.

Somehow they got her into Lampton's car and drove up the combe and along the cliff road to his rambling old farmhouse. It was raining and Abbie was reminded of her arrival in Linstowel and the drive to the cottage in Daniel's old car. She felt a terrible need for Daniel's presence. No wonder Margo came running back to him when she was ill. His capable hands, his deep voice, his innate kindness would be instant reassurance.

Lampton's place was about half a mile across country from the cottage, ideal for a hideout for two or three days. Lampton had most of his meals with his sister-in-law in the village and someone came once a week to clean the house. The farm workers rarely came into the house, so Abbie felt a sense of respite as she made up a bed in the spare room and ran a hot bath. It was hard work persuading Margo to rouse herself enough to get into it and once in its warmth she had to be almost forcibly removed and dried. Abbie's face was hot, but her sympathies nonetheless deep as she realised that this was probably Daniel's task she was undertaking.

Lampton was in a mood to reject the whole idea.

"I don't know why I'm doing this—why I've allowed

myself to get involved—" he fumed as Abbie prepared a scratch meal in his enormous kitchen.

"To protect Ghislaine," Abbie reminded him shortly. "And more indirectly to protect Paul and Peter Enys— maybe even save the school."

He was silent, pacing up and down.

Abbie put scrambled eggs on toast and sat down at one end of the big kitchen table. "You'll have to take me down to the school very early tomorrow, but please come straight back. Margo needs constant watching."

"Don't worry," he said grudgingly. "If I'm going to do it I'll do the job properly. How long for?"

"Just tomorrow and Friday. Then we'll take her into Casterbridge. I think I can talk her into getting treatment once she's properly rested."

Abbie's optimism was for Lampton's benefit only, and her plans stopped dead at Saturday morning. She spent a trying night on a camp bed in Margo's room, awakened from an uneasy sleep every so often by mutterings and agonised shouts from the wrecked human being in the bed.

The next two days had a curious dream-like quality. Abbie blessed her previous good organisation at the school, because now it ran by itself while she moved automatically from task to task. Lampton collected her at four-thirty on Thursday afternoon and brought her back at seven the next morning. She had just made herself tea and toast when the telephone rang in the study.

"Abbie," it was Daniel. Her heart was in her mouth. "Where were you last night? I kept ringing until past midnight."

She parried his question. "Why? Was something the matter with the boys?"

"No. They said they thought you were ill. You told Peter you had a headache."

"Oh. Yes. I went to bed early. I took the phone off the hook."

"It was ringing through all right. Abbie, what's wrong?"

"Nothing. I did feel rather peculiar—I must have thought I took the telephone off. Anyway, I slept through it ringing." That was true at any rate. "Daniel, I have to go. Everything's fine. Thanks for ringing." She replaced the receiver quickly. She could not trust herself to lie to Daniel.

School went on as the day before. Lady Margaret turned up unexpectedly in the afternoon and took the little ones for reading. "I just wanted to be with you all," she said in her deep voice. Unfortunately she showed signs of wanting to stay on with Abbie after school had finished. Abbie took her across to the school house and stood indecisively looking at the unlit fire, wondering whether it would be quicker to offer her tea or not. She had hoped to have some time to herself before Lampton arrived. Maybe to ring up Steve. Maybe just to think about what was to be done.

Lady Margaret took up her stance with her back to the grate.

"No tea, thank you, Mrs Eliot. I have to get back to the Hall to meet my solicitors."

"Oh?" Abbie sat on the edge of a chair and wondered if Margo had got up today. She had dressed herself last night and come downstairs for an hour to sit staring moodily into the fire, but she had been asleep when Abbie left that morning.

"Yes. I would like you to be among the first to hear my news, my dear. I think of you as a friend already."

Abbie's attention was finally caught. She looked at the upright figure standing with legs apart on her hearth. Was Lady Margaret going to tell her she could no longer help at the school?

"I had an offer in the summer from a firm of holiday camps. They wanted to buy the Hall and grounds. Turn it into a holiday camp—they called it a village. You can imagine my reply!" Lady Margaret gave a snort of laughter. "I couldn't imagine it—my family have lived at the Hall since Norman times. Well, not quite." She gave what amounted to a conspiratorial wink in Abbie's direction. "But then . . . well, Mrs Eliot, I'm very short of money. I'd have had to sell eventually. And this way, I bring new blood into Linstowel." She straightened her straight back still further. "I've talked to other people, got expert advice, that sort of thing. It seems this holiday business is quite an industry. Even in the winter the chalets are occupied. So I saw the firm again and stipulated that all staff must be local people—"

"Lady Margaret—" Abbie had jumped to her feet.

178

"This is the most wonderful news. You do realise that what you're doing is to save Linstowel?"

"Oh, my dear child. You make me sound like Grace Darling or someone." The deprecating laugh was deep and husky. "But it does make the loss of my home more acceptable, I'll admit. And actually they are supplying me with an excellent house, all mod. cons. Between you and me, the Hall is very cold and uncomfortable in the winter. And I can't afford staff any more."

Abbie postponed all thoughts of Lampton and Margo and made tea in a triumphal mood, and she and Lady Margaret toasted Linstowel's glowing future solemnly. Now that the decision had been made and confided to someone, Lady Margaret was in high spirits, the years seemed to fall away from her and she walked the two yards of hearth rug making hypothetical plans for expanding the village and organising fishing trips on a grand scale. Abbie smiled, watching her. It was good to know that this was one difficulty solved, and so magnificently solved. Lampton would be delighted . . . where was Lampton?

At last Lady Margaret left to meet her solicitors and Mrs Thompson had her usual Friday cup of tea and departed. Abbie glanced at her watch. It was half-past five, already dark, and no signs of Lampton's dusty old car.

At last the telephone rang.

"Mrs Eliot—" Abbie recognised the belligerent voice with relief. "She's gone. Margo Ritchie. I went up with a cup of tea before I left and there's no sign of her."

Abbie was incredulous. "You'd have seen her—"

"I was doing book work all afternoon in the office. She could have gone through the front door—I've searched all the outbuildings—"

"The cottage. Or the halt. Maybe she's trying to get back to London."

"No trains now."

"She wouldn't think of that. I'll go there. You go to the cottage."

"Right. I'll drive straight down to you afterwards." For once he sounded eager to help.

Abbie grabbed her coat and a torch and half-ran, half-walked up the lane towards the halt. She did not know whether to be appalled or not at Lampton's news. Perhaps Margo had felt her old self during the day and made her own plans; she was still an individual with her own rights and in a way it would solve Abbie's immediate problem if she had decided to go back to London. But it was only the immediate problem. In the turmoil of the last two days Abbie had not forgotten Margo's agonised confession that she was in love with Daniel. In her right mind, Margo apparently had enough self-control to try to let him lead his own life, but once she was ill, her need for Daniel blotted out all else. Until she was finally cured, she would be coming back to Linstowel at shorter and shorter intervals.

It took about three minutes to discover that Margo was not at the halt. Abbie flashed her torch around the old waiting-room and up and down the platforms. It was beginning to rain again, no wet footprints in the waiting-room except her own. She hurried back home as fast as she could to find Lampton waiting for her.

"Good riddance," he said as he followed her into the cold sitting-room.

"I hoped she'd be here. I left the kitchen door open . . ." Abbie looked at him helplessly. "What now?"

"Forget her. Until next time. If she's well enough to walk out to the Castle Combe road and hitch a lift— and that's what she must have done—then she's not going to worry us any more, is she?"

"Poor Margo." Abbie sagged suddenly into a chair. Now that the grinding need to deal with the situation seemed over, she could understand that thin, shivering figure so much better. "She's an artist—a good one apparently. She must be living in a particularly ghastly sort of hell. And she doesn't want to be cured because then she'd probably never see Daniel again."

Lampton was seized with the same retrospective mood. He said grimly, staring into the empty grate, "She poisoned Ghislaine's mind against me. That's why I hated her. Without her always poking fun at me I might have stood a chance. . . . There was a time when Ghislaine loved me . . ."

Abbie looked at him sharply. Why had he used the past tense when he spoke of hating Margo? With a queer tight feeling in her throat, she thought—he's as unbalanced as Margo when it comes to Ghislaine.

The telephone stammered into the silence that was suddenly tense. It was Daniel. Abbie was so pleased to hear his voice she almost sobbed. It seemed incredible

181

neither she nor Lampton had thought of the obvious place to look for Margo.

"Abbie, what's wrong—are you crying?" Daniel's voice was irritable with anxiety.

"Yes. I'm fine now. Is Margo with you?"

"Of course. She's told me how good you've been. Abbie, we must talk. Something's happened—it's ridiculous, yet we must sort it out. Can you dry your eyes like a good girl and come to the inn straightaway?" He sounded tender, almost light-hearted.

"Oh, Daniel, we've been looking for her and I was so frightened something might have happened. I'll tell you later."

"Is Lampton with you?" his voice sharpened.

"Yes, of course. He's been to the cottage and I've been to the halt—"

"Stay where you are. I'll be there—I'll bring Margo and be with you in five minutes." The phone clicked its full stop.

"What was all that about?" Lampton said behind her. "Do I gather that woman is at the Lobster Pot? After all that—"

"She's coming here. In five minutes—with Daniel."

Abbie pushed past him and knelt to light the fire. Then she went through into the kitchen and laid a tray while the coffee heated. She realised she'd had nothing since school lunch and the thought of seeing Daniel again put her whole world in order, so that she noticed she was hungry and thirsty and cold. Her sudden and startling suspicion of poor Lampton made her want to laugh now. She forced him into a chair and put a mug of coffee into his hands.

Daniel's old Morris drew up before she could drink hers. She opened the door and took Margo's hands to lead her to the fire. The white face was still painfully drawn, but the dark eyes were quiet and it was plain Margo was once again in control of herself. She avoided Lampton's scornful look and held out her hands to the new flames in the hearth. Daniel followed closely and sat down in a chair he pulled up between her and Lampton. He put a protective arm across her shoulders.

"Thanks, Abbie." He took some coffee from the proffered tray and held it out to Margo. "Come along. Drink this. It's cold outside and you've been coddled in bed for the last two days."

"In *my* house," snapped Lampton.

Margo flashed at him, "Only because you thought you had to. Abbie helped through common humanity. And I think Daniel has in the past even though . . . even though . . ." She looked at him pleadingly.

"Hush, Margo. We've been through all that. You're a person well worth looking after. You must build up your self-respect again . . ."

"Well, has she agreed to go into hospital and get herself cured once and for all," asked Lampton brusquely. "Or are we going to repeat this charade two or three times a year?"

"She's going into hospital," Daniel replied quietly. "But first of all we're going to tell our stories to Abbie.

183

She's the only one who can be at once sympathetic and objective towards all of us. I want her to hear what happened the night Ghislaine died."

Lampton stood up. "If we're muck-raking, I'm off. There's enough of that in this village without us joining in—"

"Sit down, Lampton!" Daniel barked. "We particularly need your version." Lampton looked at Daniel's burly figure and sat down again reluctantly. Daniel went on in a soft voice, "I'm going to start, but I can't go far. Margo will come after. Then you, Lampton. He took his arm away from Margo's shoulders, sipped his coffee and began. "Ghislaine had several affairs. I no longer loved her and I couldn't believe she loved me. But we still had our family. I told her she was to stay at home in future, I was selling the cottage and she'd have no more weekends up there." His voice was quite flat and expressionless. Abbie shivered, imagining the rows, Ghislaine's beauty which probably made even her defiance magnificent, Daniel's lacerated feelings. "On that night in April, she told me she was going to the cottage whether I liked it or not. She'd been drinking but I didn't think she was drunk. I assumed she was meeting someone there—I didn't know about you, Lampton. It was only later when your sister-in-law started talking that I realised you ᵣ . . knew Ghislaine. Anyway, she went. People tell me I threatened to kill her. But she still went." He took a deep breath. "Go on, Margo."

"Nobody knew I was at the cottage except Ghislaine.

She used to let me stay there when I was ill just as I do now. She told me she was leaving Daniel and going off with Charlie Lampton—he'd promised to sell the farm and all his land. He had more money than Daniel would ever have. I told her she was mad. I called Charlie names—I never could understand how she could consider Charlie after Daniel. But it was the money. We had a blazing row and I told her to run off to her Punch and Judy man straightaway. She said that was exactly what she intended to do and she stormed out of the cottage. It was dark and raining. I stood and listened to her running across the field and I was still there when she started screaming." Margo put her hands to her face. "She screamed for a long time, then there was a pause and a long-drawn-out scream. I knew what had happened. She'd gone over the cliff." The long artist's hands fell into her lap. "All this time I've thought Daniel killed her. I thought he must have followed her. I could imagine her taunting him with her desertion and his sudden blazing temper. I went away then so that I wouldn't have to implicate him. Later, I had to see him. He was pretending it was an accident and something in me—some devil—couldn't let it rest at that. I was frightened to tell him what I thought was the truth, so I told him he was responsible for her death—indirectly. I told him she was an alcoholic like me, that I'd been at the cottage that night and seen her drinking. That she had set off back home intending to beg his forgiveness. I don't know why I did it . . ." She stopped and buried her face in her hands.

185

Daniel put a hand on her shoulder. "Go on, Margo. Finish."

She said hesitantly, "When I'm—ill—it doesn't seem so bad. I reason that there is no happiness for him, he's a murderer, so I might as well gain what little comfort—"

"No, Margo. Go on from today."

She visibly pulled herself together. "It was today I discovered that Charlie Lampton had found Ghislaine's body that night." She spoke directly to Abbie. "I was on my way to the inn last Wednesday, as usual. Then I felt so ill, I was just by the school, and I knew you were partially in Daniel's confidence, so I thought I could rest for an hour or so. When you started organising things to save Daniel, I thought, why not? It all seemed rather funny at the time. Like watching a play." She paused. "It's no good apologising. I shall do it all again. The next time." Abbie looked at the long fingers clasping and unclasping. Somehow or other, whatever the consequences, Margo had to get some proper treatment. . . . "Funnily enough, I felt better at Charlie's place. I suppose at the cottage I'm hating myself all the time for torturing Daniel. I didn't feel guilty about you two, not in the same way. Then, last night you were talking while I was downstairs. Charlie was grumbling about me—as usual. What trash I was compared with Ghislaine. You tried to shut him up, Abbie, and he said something about Ghislaine being beautiful even when she was lying in the cove battered to pieces. You said—that's enough, Mr Lampton—in your stern teacher voice—" For a moment a smile touched Margo's lips and was gone. "And I began to think. I asked you later who had found Ghislaine's body and you looked surprised and said it was Lampton. I thought about it all morning. Lampton was there along that cliff that April night, probably coming up to the cottage to see Ghislaine. When he was in his study this afternoon, I decided to go. I was frightened." She glanced at Abbie again and said in her flat monotone, "Lampton hates me."

Abbie looked across at Lampton. He was red and furious.

"What is this—some private court? I'm not sitting listening to this rubbish any longer! I tried to help this woman—"

Abbie said quietly, "You felt bound to help her, Mr Lampton. Why? You knew Ghislaine was no alcoholic and everyone knows you were in love with her. So you had no reason to protect her or yourself. Why did you tell me she was an alcoholic? Just one more reason why she fell off that cliff?" Lampton said nothing. Abbie went on quietly, almost inaudibly, "Ghislaine is dead, but she has left misery in her wake. Maybe she would rest more peacefully if you told us what really happened that night."

Another silence. Daniel turned impatiently to face Lampton, but Abbie held up her hand and he said nothing. At last Lampton began to speak. His voice was weary, resigned.

"All right. It'll do no good. If the law could have punished me I would have given myself up immediately.

All that your precious truth will do now is to make life unbearable for the rest of the Enys family. I didn't kill her. But if I hadn't been there, she wouldn't have died." He glanced at Margo. "If it's any comfort to you, your words had great effect on Ghislaine that night. Somewhere along the cliff she decided you were right and she'd try again with her family. She met me on my way up to see her. I had made plans, bought air tickets for Italy. I was so—happy. She told me it was all off for the moment, but she'd see me again in about six months. I said I couldn't go on like this, my life was a see-saw of hope and despair. She started to laugh—she wouldn't stop. She said I was like Punch in more ways than one and she could never learn the part of Judy. I tried to persuade her to go back to the cottage where we could talk properly—it was raining hard. We . . . grappled. I think I might have hit her—I don't know. I can't remember now. She kept screaming and I tried to stop her. Then she broke away from me and started to run. I ran after her, but I didn't touch her again. It was muddy. She went over the cliff like a seal."

Abbie put out a hand and touched the bowed head. So much of Lampton was explained. His fierce determination to keep the village alive was all part of his obsession with Ghislaine. The curious mixture of his concern for the little Enys twins and his hatred of Daniel was now clear. He was right, if all this sordid business had come under the glare of publicity, it would have been hard for them all.

She said softly, "Let her rest now, Charlie. She did

such a lot of damage in her brief life. Let her go . . . go
right away from Linstowel and forget her."

He looked up at her as if she had offered him a gift.
"Can any of us forget her?" he said.

"Of course. You've released Daniel and Margo tonight by what you've said. Release yourself. You could
never have been happy with Ghislaine—you must have
known that all the time. Her death gave you a second
chance. Take it."

He turned to Daniel and Margo. "It wasn't only to
protect myself, you know, that I kept quiet. It was
mostly Ghislaine. And her sons."

Daniel nodded. "We understand more than anyone
else. But I'm glad we know now."

"Mrs Eliot says I've released you. Is that true?"

Margo said, "My love for Daniel isn't evil any more.
I might be able to cope with it. If I can keep well and
work . . ."

"You'll go into hospital?" Abbie said swiftly.

Margo smiled briefly. "You do like everything to be
neat and tidy, Abbie, don't you? Will you move in with
Daniel now and tidy him up?" She noticed Abbie's
flinch and went on, "I'm sorry, my dear, that wasn't
meant as a gibe. . . . Yes, I'll go into hospital and
when I come out I'll visit Linstowel and do a portrait
of you all."

Other things were said, meaningless things, because
now that they had bared their souls there was a certain
constraint and embarrassment. Abbie went upstairs to
make up a bed for Margo and when she came down

Lampton had left. She took Margo upstairs and settled her with a light meal on a tray. In the morning Lampton had promised to drive her into Casterbridge. Daniel would go as well and Abbie said she would take over the twins for the day. Margo was pathetically grateful and the idea of Casterbridge hospital with Daniel and Abbie able to visit her every week was not nearly as frightening as London. She was very tired and she held Abbie's hand as she passed over the tray.

"I wonder what would have happened to us all if you had never taken the job at Linstowel?"

Abbie whispered, "Go to sleep. I've done nothing—"

"You were here. And you listened. I envy those kids up at the school. . . ." The eyelids drooped and Abbie crept from the room.

Downstairs Daniel was waiting. He held out his arms and Abbie went into them and put her head thankfully on to his shoulder. "So much to talk about," she murmured.

"And so much time, my dearest." Daniel leaned back to look at her. "I'm going to court you properly, Abbie. As befits a widower courting a widow. We will have long hours out walking to talk about everything that has happened. We can tidy it up if you like. But it will never be very civilised, my darling."

She looked at him steadily, searching his dark face, the unquiet eyes, the shock of hair. "There is nothing very civilised about our love either, Daniel. Sometimes it frightens me."

He held her close. "I know. I can feel you wanting

190

to run when I come near. But it is real, Abbie. It is vital and alive."

"It is why I can accept Mark and Christopher's death," she whispered into his jumper.

"It has given me new life, Abbie." He kissed her hair. "Even before I knew about Lampton—when I still believed I was directly responsible for Ghislaine's death —I was beginning to live again. I've got bookings for the Christmas holiday—I want to give a party—"

"Oh, Daniel," she was weeping. "So much energy—"

"So much to do," he murmured. And his arms held her tightly as he kissed her.